Black-eyed Suzie

Black-eyed Suzie

by

Susan Shaw

Front Street
Asheville, North Carolina

Acknowledgments

With many thanks to Greg Linder and Sandra Kring

Copyright © 2002 by Susan Shaw
Printed in China
First Front Street paperback edition, 2007

The Library of Congress has cataloged the hardcover edition of this book as follows:

Library of Congress Cataloging-in-Publication Data

Shaw, Susan.
Black-eyed Suzie / by Susan Shaw. — 1st ed.
[168] p. :   cm.
Summary: Suzie's stay in a mental hospital helps her tear down the walls of a
devastating psychological prison she calls "the box."
ISBN: 1-56397-729-X
1. Mothers and daughters — Fiction — Juvenile literature. 2. Mental illness —
Fiction — Juvenile literature. (1. Mothers and daughters — Fiction. 2. Mental
illness — Fiction.) I. Title.
[F]   21   2002   AC   CIP
2001091725
Paperback ISBN 978-1-59078-533-1

Front Street
An Imprint of Boyds Mills Press, Inc.
A Highlights Company
815 Church Street
Honesdale, Pennsylvania 18431

To John, Janet, Ben, and Warren
with love

✳✳✳

I live in a box with four sides, tall and brown. I cannot get out.

Sometimes I do get out. Not my body. Just my mind. That's when I'm on my cloud of different shades of pink. My body stays in the box, but the cloud takes me higher and higher until I'm just a little brown dot in a brown box.

It's peaceful and cool on my cloud. Sometimes I think the cloud will take me so far away I'll never have to come back. That would be the best thing. That's what I try for.

From my cloud I look down at my twelve-year-old self, sitting quietly in my box. I do it so well.

❋

In my box, I sit in a chair and watch my mother reupholster the easy chair in the living room. She is good at putting in the tacks. One by one, she takes them out from between her lips with her fingers and taps them into place with her hammer. Mom is good at reupholstering. She's good at wallpapering, too. She wallpapered the living room last year. She picked the curvy, golden design and made the drapes to match. She's good at lots of things.

After each tack goes into the chair, Mom looks at me.

"Do something, Suzie," she says finally. "Don't just sit there."

I don't answer. She knows I can't talk.

Mom doesn't see the box. I know this, even as I know that there is one. It feels like there's always been a box. It's just that lately the walls are close, pushing against me on all sides. I have no room, and my knees are up at my chin.

So I just sit here. There's nothing else I can do. Mom must know that. I'm pretty good at sitting quietly, though, most of the time. It doesn't bother anyone. Not usually.

Right now it's bothering Mom. "You're stupid, sitting there. Go upstairs where I can't see you."

It's like scalding steam coming out of her mouth, making my eyes run. Oh, I'm crying. Mom gets angry when I cry.

She pushes hard against one of my chair legs, so hard I rock and almost fall. But the chair settles. The box presses against me tighter. I sit so still, so still.

"I hate you, crying like that. Go upstairs."

What she says hurts me like bee stings on my face. It's my fault that she's angry. It's my fault that I make her hate me. But I wish she didn't.

Under the hate, I know she loves me.

I want to stop crying so I can please her, but I can't. I'm so tired. Sitting here like this takes all my energy. I can't find any more to push back the tears.

"Oh, Lord," Mom says. She puts the finished chair into the corner and cleans up the mess. Carrying the hammer and some trash, she leaves the room, her quick steps banging against the wooden floor. They echo back to me from the rear of the house.

Dad opens the door. With him is Uncle Elliot. I'm surprised to see Uncle Elliot, even though he's Dad's boss. He hasn't been here since he and Mom had that argument last winter. I don't want him to see me like this. I try to sit invisibly in my box, but I'm still crying.

"Why, Suzie," Uncle Elliot asks first thing. "Are you sick?" Uncle Elliot rests his palm on my forehead for a moment. "No fever," he says. "Stomachache? What, Suzie?"

Dad looks uncomfortable, like he wishes I would cry somewhere else so Uncle Elliot wouldn't see.

"Why don't you answer?" Uncle Elliot asks me. "Is it your throat?"

Mom comes back. She jumps when she sees Uncle Elliot.

"He's just here to pick up that package, Corynne," says Dad.

Mom's biting her lower lip. She's still mad at me, I can tell, and she doesn't like it that Uncle Elliot is here. She talks nice in front of him, though. She even strokes my hair. I like that. I lean my head against her breast. Warm and soft. It feels so good when Mom is nice.

But I still cry. I can't help it.

"It's okay, Elliot." Dad's voice is reassuring and warm. "Corynne and I have it under control."

"What are you talking about? Suzie's sick. She needs a doctor!"

I don't like them talking about me and looking at me. I try to find my cloud, but I can't think that hard with the crying and Uncle Elliot being here and all the attention.

"It's really all right, Elliot." Dad's looking nervous, pulling on his tie, shooting little glances at Mom. "She's just going through a stage."

"A stage!" thunders Uncle Elliot. "A stage? I never saw a stage like this in any of my daughters."

"You didn't raise one like Suzie," Mom says. "Suzie's different. Suzie's strange."

Uncle Elliot stares at Mom. "Look at her," he says. "Look at the circles under her eyes. When was the last time she ate? Or smiled? Or talked? And her hair . . ."

I can't comb my hair, I want to explain. You can't do that when you have to sit so still. And smiling takes so much energy . . .

Mom and Dad look at each other.

"This is just her way," says Mom. "She's like this."

"Bull!"

I jump at Uncle Elliot's roar. He swings to face Dad. "Lift up your daughter. I'll drive her in my car."

"Now wait a minute." Mom walks away from me, then turns so I can see her face.

Oh, no, oh, no. Her right eye is twitching. And her voice is high and loud, shriller with each word. It hurts my ears. Uncle Elliot's eyebrows go way up at her tone. It's louder than last winter. I can't get my breath . . .

"You have no right, Elliot." My ears hurt so much they ring. "Suzie stays right where she is."

Uncle Elliot doesn't answer. Under his gaze, my arms and legs get pressed in closer and closer by the walls of the box. Then he looks at Mom and Dad. He whispers something, but I still hear it.

"No doctor, no job." Then he stands back, his arms crossed, and waits.

"Corynne?" Dad's voice is barely more than a whisper.

"It's an act," Mom says, waving her hand in my direction without looking at me. "She's just trying to get attention."

"Hah!" from Uncle Elliot. He stands there, his arms still crossed. His face is stern and hard, like it was carved in stone.

"Okay," says Mom after a long pause. "Elliot doesn't believe us, but he'll see. It'll be a complete waste of money to take Suzie to the hospital, but if he wants to throw his money around like that, we'll do it. We won't be gone long."

Uncle Elliot strides to the front door and opens it. "Let's go," he says.

Dad picks me up from my chair, my golden upholstered chair. The box goes, too, of course, but I want my chair.

How can I sit without it? Dad holds me, one arm under my shoulders, the other under my knees. He carries me out the door. My head flops against his arm.

I don't want to go. I want my chair. I need my chair.

Deanna, my sixteen-year-old sister, meets us on the porch steps.

"What's wrong?" She pushes my hair away from my face. All I can see are her dark-blue eyes. They're afraid. "Did something happen?"

"We're getting her checked out," says Dad cheerfully. "Uncle Elliot's idea."

Deanna brushes my cheek softly with her hand, and we leave.

"Feel better, Suzie," she calls from the porch.

＊＊＊

I had a bike when I was seven. It was pink and blue, just like the sky at sunset, and it had pink and blue plastic streamers that drooped from the handlebars. I loved those streamers. I'd run my fingers through them, warm and smooth and soft, letting them sparkle in the afternoon sun as they dropped. But I couldn't ride the bike. I was afraid.

"Don't let go! Don't let go!" I'd yell to Deanna. She would hold onto my seat and run alongside.

Deanna would never let go if I was scared. Only I couldn't stop being scared. So I stopped trying to ride. Walking was good enough for me.

Then, one afternoon, Uncle Elliot stopped by. Dad wasn't home yet, so he sat on the porch to wait for him. "How's the bike?" he asked me.

Mom's high, clear soprano painted the street from the living room while we talked.

Hush, little baby, don't say a word . . .

I shrugged.

Papa's gonna buy you a mockingbird . . .

"I can't get used to it," I said to Uncle Elliot. "The bike wobbles."

"Scared?"

"Kind of."

And if that mockingbird don't sing . . .

"That's the way I used to be. Come on. I'll get you riding."

I didn't want to. I'd given up on it. But I pushed my bike out of the garage and met Uncle Elliot on the sidewalk anyway. We couldn't make out Mom's words anymore, but her voice floated over the street like the smell of blueberry pie baking in the oven. I loved listening to it.

"Now here's what you have to do," said Uncle Elliot. "You have to think like you're an eagle."

I nodded up at him. "I'm an eagle."

"Right. And eagles fly. They don't think about it. They just do it. They know they can fly."

I closed my eyes while Uncle Elliot talked. I was an eagle, flying with pink and blue wings. I was a blur. I could do it. I *would* do it!

I opened my eyes and got on my bike. I wanted to be a pink and blue blur.

Uncle Elliot held onto my seat and ran alongside like Deanna did. At first I was wobbly, like usual.

A new eagle might be wobbly at first, I told myself.

I kept on going, pedaling faster. Wind pressed on my face, whistled in my ears. I'd never felt that on my bike.

"You're doing great!" shouted Uncle Elliot.

I pedaled faster. The hair rose from my shoulders to hang on the wind. It felt so good I didn't ever want to stop. But I had to. I ran out of sidewalk.

That's when I saw Uncle Elliot wasn't with me. I turned around. He was two houses down, laughing. "I can't run that fast," he called.

I rode back to him. I was laughing, too.

"Suzie," said Uncle Elliot, "that was great. Nothing will ever stop you now. You can do anything. You're an eagle."

※ ※ ※

The click of the turn signal with its *now, now, now* rhythm underlines how quiet it is in Uncle Elliot's car. *Now, now, now.* Right in rhythm with my crying.

I can't stop. I feel like a dam has burst and I will never stop crying. Mom and Dad cry, too. I try not to look. Nobody's saying anything, but Uncle Elliot's mouth is a firm, straight line, set hard against the smile creases in his cheeks.

My cloud floats overhead. It lifts me away. I look down and see myself huddled in my box against the rear door of Uncle Elliot's car, away from Mom. Mom is wringing her hands and shaking her head. Even though she's crying, she looks mad. I wish she wouldn't be mad. I know it's my fault, but I didn't mean for this to happen. If I could only have sat better on my chair, quietly, so quietly.

Dad looks back at me every minute. His face is sad and long. He looks angry, too, but mostly embarrassed. He wants to look good for Uncle Elliot. This doesn't look good.

My fault again. But why couldn't I be allowed to just sit quietly? I wasn't hurting anyone. Why couldn't they leave me alone?

If I wasn't so tired, I could stop crying. But I'm always, always tired.

I lie back on the cloud, let the pinkness surround me and take me high above my box.

Uncle Elliot stops the car. Dad helps me out of my seat.

I try to stay on the cloud, but it slips away. I half walk, and Dad and Mom half drag me to the building. Bryn Mawr Hospital, says the sign.

Inside, a bunch of people poke at me and ask me questions, but I find the cloud again and stay on it. They stick a plastic tube with a needle on one end into my arm. *Ouch!* That hurts. I have to leave my cloud for a second and taste the room. Cold metal, funny smells.

"IV," someone says, but then I'm away again, keeping my mind blank.

I have to keep my mind blank. I have to stay in the box. I have to sit quietly. This is how my life works. If I don't do these things, I will die.

"IV" probably means food. I haven't eaten in days, except some tomato slices that I slipped down yesterday before I started to choke. But I'm not hungry.

✳ ✳ ✳

We're back in Uncle Elliot's car. I hope we're going home, but I don't think so. Dad's head is bowed, buried in his hands. Mom's face is tight and angry.

"Look what you've done," she whispers from the seat next to me. I know she wants to hit me, but Uncle Elliot is watching in the rearview mirror. "All this trouble you've caused."

I was sitting quietly in my chair before Uncle Elliot got there. It was the best I could do. Why don't they let me go back to my chair? I'll be good. I promise. Mom could still sing and make things for the house. Maybe she wouldn't be mad at me if I sat better, a little straighter, a little quieter. I'd do that. She'd hardly know I was there.

"Leave her alone, Corynne." Uncle Elliot's voice cuts through my thoughts. "She needs help."

"Huh!" Mom pulls a tissue out of her purse. "It's a game she's playing. Can't you see?" She wipes her eyes with quivery hands.

I don't know what she means. I'm not playing a game.

Uncle Elliot shakes his head.

"It's no game," he says. "It's life. Dangerous life."

❋❋❋

I'm at St. Dorothy's. It's a mental hospital. I know, because I listen when they check me in.

Mom's so angry. I've never seen her so angry. Her hands are shaking, her right eye is twitching, and she can hardly sit still. I know she wants to hit me and yell at me for causing so much trouble, but she won't do that in front of the doctor.

Dad's angry, too. His eyebrows are drawn together, and he keeps clearing his throat. Uncle Elliot is gone. I don't know when he left.

"If we don't do this, Corynne," Dad says, "she could die." Mom doesn't answer, just presses her lips together tight.

Dr. Blackstone, a red-haired lady in a white coat, gives Mom a curious look.

"I still say we can take care of her at home," Mom says.

"Ma'am," says the doctor, "how are you going to get her to eat?"

An unwelcome memory floods over me. One dinnertime when I was four, I couldn't eat my mashed sweet potatoes. I hated them. Just looking at them made me gag.

Mom told me I couldn't leave my seat until they were gone. Then she left the kitchen. So I sat there alone with the orange mound in front of me, while Mom practiced her singing in the living room. I sat there a long time. But I couldn't eat those sweet potatoes.

The kitchen dropped into shadow at sunset, and I was still there at the table. Mom stopped singing, and I could hear her talking on the phone. Finally, I tipped my fork to the yucky stuff and brought the barest touch to my mouth. It wasn't so-o-o bad that way.

That's when Mom came back into the kitchen. "I think I'm getting to like sweet potatoes," I told her. I wanted to please her. I really did.

But she must have had a hard day. She looked at my full plate and snapped. One fast forkful after another, she stuffed the sweet potatoes into my mouth. My spine arched against the high seat back, my hands useless against my mother's force. I couldn't talk, I couldn't breathe, I couldn't resist.

If I could only have swallowed, but there was never enough time. In, in, in it came, until it was all gone.

"I'm going to throw up," I said when she was finished.

"You better not."

But I did. All over the bathroom floor. Crying.

But that was a long time ago. She wouldn't do that again.

I don't care about food, anyway. It doesn't matter. I'm not hungry.

I don't want to be here. I can sit in a chair at home just as well as here. That's what I'm going to do, no matter where I am. It's all I can do. Why can't I do it at home? No one would care.

If I hadn't started crying . . .

If Uncle Elliot hadn't come in just then, I'd still be at home. Why did he have to come in and change everything?

Mom and Dad get up from their red chairs with the chrome armrests. Dad pats me on the top of my head. Mom sails out the door ahead of him without looking at me.

"Corynne!"

Where are they going?

I'm alone with the doctor. She looks at me from her desk, the eyes behind her glasses wide and sad and knowing, her mouth turned down. Why is she sad? What does she know?

Then she smiles at me. "Try not to worry, Suzie," she says "You're in good hands."

My parents—where did they go?

Dr. Blackstone picks up a green phone. "Jody?" she says into it.

A lady in a light-green outfit comes in. Her name tag says Jody. She's all chatty, talking about my blonde hair like it's pretty, and what a cute blue outfit I have on. She doesn't know it's just an old one of my sister's. It matches *her* eyes, not my black ones. Deanna's the pretty one.

Jody helps me to my feet. I can see out the window. I see them. I see Mom and Dad getting into our turquoise van. How did it get here?

Wait! They're leaving me. How can they do that?

I shiver and don't stop. My tears come big with harsh gasps. I don't know this place. I don't know these people. I feel like a rowboat dropped onto the middle of a stormy ocean. I'm going to die. I pull my box close around me like an old worn-out sweater, but that doesn't help. I can't find my cloud, either.

"Come on, honey." Jody's voice is sweet and slow-moving, like a lazy river. "Don't take on so. You'll be fine."

Fine? I'm going to die.

I want to go home.

Something's wrong with my legs. They hold me up okay, but I can't make them take me anywhere. I pull my feet up like they're stuck in some kind of syrup, but they come right down again where I stand.

"Oh, my," says Jody. "You *are* in a bad way."

She takes my arm. Her hands are warm and dark. I look at her face, also dark, set with wide, caring eyes. She pulls me down a bright hallway with huge blue and white squares of linoleum tile on the floor. I don't resist her, but I can't help her, either. My feet in their sandals go *shh-shh, shh-shh,* never leaving the floor.

We meet another lady in a green outfit. She looks at me like she knows something about me and is sorry. *What?* I want to ask. *Why are you sorry?*

"Want some help, Jody?"

"No," says Jody. "We're doing fine."

Jody steers me into a room with a bed.

I don't like beds. Beds are only for sleep. If you don't sleep, they just make you feel bad. But that's where Jody puts me. I sit while she takes off my sandals and clothes before slipping me into a cold white nightgown. Then she tips my head back onto the pillow and lifts my feet onto the bed. Automatically, I bring my knees high under my chin while she pulls up the sheet. The bed feels good against my stiff back, but why bother? I can't remember the last time I really slept.

Jody hooks my arm to another IV. More food, I guess. Jody is talking, but I'm not listening to her. There's so much noise inside my head. Why did Mom and Dad leave me here? When will they be back for me? Are they coming back at all?

"Pleasant dreams," Jody says. She leaves the room.

My heart thumps and thumps against my chest. Thoughts race a mile a minute.

I'm so scared.

※

I sit up quick. Where am I? What am I doing?

One thought dashes in after another.

I grab the white bed frame. Is this my room? Where's the window? I hear a noise, like a teakettle before it sings. It's me, breathing in short, wheezing gasps.

A lady comes into the room. It's Jody, warm, comfortable, dark. No, it's Mom, red nail polish and thin.

"Suzie? Are you okay?" She has Jody's voice.

I grab Jody's dark, thick arm. Mom has thin, white arms. I know this isn't Mom. Then I know she is. Or she's Deanna.

Wait.

Mom? Deanna? Mom? MOM?

My head feels heavy with a million whirling, speeding, storming thoughts.

Jody rocks me and rocks me. I hold her tight. She's not my mom or Deanna. I know this, but images shift nightmarishly like patches of moonlight on red and orange leaves. Nothing I see makes sense. Mom and Deanna come and go like overlays, but Jody is there every time, solid.

"You're okay, Suzie." Who's Suzie? I can't remember.

What was that name?

After a while, the images thin out until they're gone like ghosts in morning sunshine. I'm left with the stark clearness of the hospital room where, rocking and rocking, I hold on tightly to Jody.

I'm not okay. I'm scared

Jody does something to the IV in my arm. She stays with me until, for the first time in a long time, I drift off to sleep.

Morning. Sunlight streaks through the window, throwing patterns on the wall. My box is still here, but it's always here, like a turtle's shell. I'm so used to it I hardly think about it.

I'm not crying. Not crying reminds me that I never stopped crying yesterday.

Jody being Mom or Deanna comes back to me like a rush of wind. I feel like a house spun off its foundations by ocean water in a hurricane's raging surge. And I remember that I am Suzie. Aren't I?

Suzie, Suzie, Suzie. I nail the name down with my mother's upholstery tacks.

The name is gone. Suzie?

I'm at the bottom of some deep hole where I can't see to the top. I'm as far down as there is to go. How did I get down here?

I think of home. It's a place where Mom works on projects around the house and gives singing lessons. It's where sometimes Deanna's long black hair is all I see of her, she zips in and out so fast, giggling with her friends. It's where Dad's snoring rattles the house when he's not traveling. It's where I quietly sit, not bothering anyone. That's my life.

Maybe I can go home, now that I've stopped crying. I promise I won't bother anyone.

I look around the room. Next to the window, there's a

picture of a huge red flower with widely spread petals. It's so bright it almost hurts my eyes.

I want to look out the window, but when I stand up, I can't move forward. My legs still don't work. I fall back, crying into my pillow. I wish I was still sleeping.

Another lady in a green suit comes in. Her name tag reads Marie.

"Good morning, Suzie," she says. Her voice is warm and low, and I like her smile. I push back the tears. If I don't cry, maybe I can go home. "How about a trip to the bathroom?"

She helps me to my feet like she knows I can't walk. We pass the window, where I see the leaves in a weeping willow tree move in the breeze. I guess it's hot out there under the August sun. It's cool in this room, almost cold.

Marie helps me sit on the toilet. The seat is cold and hard under my bony rear end. Marie hands me toilet paper and I use it. At least I can do that. She helps me wash my hands while she hums a tune I don't know.

Marie steers me back to my bed, where breakfast is waiting on some kind of tray table. It makes me want to choke. Orange juice and toast and oatmeal. I can't stand to look at it. I close my eyes and search for the cloud.

"Come on, Suzie," says Marie. "Let's try. Just try."

I look at Marie. I know my eyes are filling up again. *Try? I can't try.*

"Have a sip of juice."

By the time she has the juice glass halfway to my mouth, I'm sobbing. She puts the juice back on the tray. "Well, okay," she says. "You can't eat when you're crying."

I wait for her to yell at me for crying, for not cooperating, but she doesn't. She doesn't even look mad. She pushes the tray table away and sits on a green, padded chair.

"Why are you crying? Because I want you to eat?"

I don't know why I'm crying. I just am.

Marie dabs my eyes and face with a tissue. I stop crying on the outside.

"Tell you what," she says. "Have the tiniest little bit of the oatmeal. They make it real good here, with cinnamon and sugar. It'll just slip right down."

She dips the spoon into the bowl, coming up with the barest coating on the tip. I don't want it. I know I'll choke.

She waits with the spoon until I'm ready. I'll never be ready, but I open my mouth.

In goes the spoon, onto my tongue. I choke. Marie's right there with the napkin. "It's okay," she says. "I'm glad you tried. We'll forget the toast, but try to swallow some juice."

I want to please Marie. She's a nice person. She didn't get mad at me for not cooperating. I watch her ladle out a little juice with the spoon. Hardly anything. But it doesn't matter. I'll never get it down.

"Sometime," she says, coming nearer, "I want you to tell me what your favorite ice cream is."

Strawberry, I'm thinking. I used to love strawberry ice cream with the big frozen strawberry chunks. I'm thinking about that when the spoon empties into my mouth. Marie tilts my head so the juice won't spill out. I choke.

Marie's ready with the napkin, catching most of the yellow liquid. I wait for her to be mad, to say that I did it on purpose. "All right!" she exclaims, like I scored a touchdown. "Good job!"

Good job? I spit up half of what she gave me. I think she's crazy. Then I remember I'm the crazy person. Otherwise, why am I here?

"You'll eat more next time." She says that like she knows, but I know she's wrong. She hooks me back into the IV.

"Breakfast," she says, tapping the plastic tube. "Ham and eggs today."

I look at her.

"That's a joke, Suzie."

I smile, sort of. It's like working dry clay.

"Hey!" Marie claps her hands. "Ten points for smiling!"

She whisks away the tray, and I stay there on the bed with ham and eggs and something that lets me sleep whirling into my blood.

＊＊＊

Scared. Sobbing, heart racing. I hardly notice where a man as tall as a doorway is steering me. *I want to go home! I want to go home!*

The giant helps me into a chair with a green cushion. "Here's the doc," he tells me, nodding at the red-haired lady from yesterday. Her white coat opens over a blue dress.

"Thanks, Bill." She sits opposite me. I hear the door close behind Bill. "Call me Stella," she says. "Everybody does."

Scared, scared, scared.

"How are you feeling this morning?"

Feeling?

"Jody said you had a bad night."

I want to go home! Why did my parents leave me?

The box is tight, and I'm sobbing through all of this. I squeeze my arms around my knees. I know I'm going to die.

"Suzie," the doctor says, "what's happening to you has happened to other people. I've seen it before, and I can help you."

Mom! I want my mom!

She leans forward, red hair falling away from her shoulders, green eyes serious behind the glasses. "You had a bad experience. I don't know what it was. Right now, I believe you don't, either. But we'll work together, and you'll remember . . ."

The gold chair. The chair. The chair.

". . . and then you'll feel better."

I hold my knees until my shoulders hurt.

I'm sitting at a table. There's music playing, someone singing "Raindrops Keep Falling on My Head." In front of me is a piece of paper and some crayons. I haven't played with crayons in a long time.

There are other kids in the room. Some of them are drawing. One of them is singing along with the tape. Another is sitting with her head down, her dark-blonde hair half-covering her eyes, her knees up at her chin. She's sitting so still, I wonder if she's breathing.

Then I realize I'm looking into a mirror.

Is that really me? I don't recognize myself with the hollows in my cheeks and the hair that's just anywhere. But the black eyes are mine. Where did I get that shirt with the black-eyed Susans on it?

Edgar, the man in charge of what we're doing, sits down next to me. The kid at the next table, a girl of about ten with a million tiny brown curls, watches him with steady, unblinking eyes.

"Don't you want to draw, Suzie?" Edgar asks.

"Look, Edgar," she calls over his words. She stands to show her paper smeared with black and purple squiggles. She's wearing a thin, outgrown dress with the waist way too high, but she's so skinny it's not tight. Under the short skirt, her legs are like poles with bony knobs halfway down.

"Very nice, Karen," Edgar answers. Then he turns back to me.

After a second, Karen sits down, still watching. She has a mad face. I don't like that mad face looking at me. I move my head so I can't see her.

Edgar puts a red crayon in my hand. I don't drop it, but I don't use it. I can't, anyhow, any more than I can talk. He picks up a black crayon and draws on the paper. I watch as the curves and lines turn into Mickey Mouse. But Edgar stops drawing before he finishes. Mickey has no mouth.

"Finish it for me," says Edgar. "You can do it."

No, I can't.

"Come on." Edgar's voice is soft, like charcoal on construction paper. "Give it a try."

Can't. Can't.

"Oh, God." Karen leaps out of her chair. She reaches across the table and draws a wide purple smile across Mickey's face. "Can't even do that, huh? Stupid." She pushes my shoulder so hard I fall off the chair.

"Karen!" There's a hard edge to Edgar's voice. He helps me back onto my seat while Bill takes Karen out of the room. "I'll get you another paper, Suzie." Edgar leaves me.

There. Quiet. I have my cloud around me, and I'm okay again. There now. There.

But Mickey Mouse taunts me with that ugly smile.

I stare at the smile, making it fade away. Then I see what belongs there. A straight line. No frown, no smile. Just a straight line. Uncle Elliot's mouth.

*** *

Mom and Deanna visit me in the solarium. Other people are here, too, doing puzzles or talking. Stella writes on a pad in the corner. Wherever you go in this place, somebody's always writing.

Deanna and Mom talk. I don't listen. When I'm on my cloud, I can't listen too hard. It's so much work just to be on it. I need to stay where it's quiet and safe.

Mom's face is mad because I'm not answering, not cooperating. I would cooperate if I could. But it's been a long time since I owned any words. That was fine at home. At least it seemed like it was. So why is Mom mad now?

Sometimes Deanna's round eyes are on the other patients, sometimes on Mom, sometimes on me. Deanna isn't saying much, but her face is sad. I know she never expected me, her little sister, to be in a place like this. Me neither, I guess. I'm not even sure why I'm here. No one tells me.

Ohh! Oww! Mom's hands are on my shoulders, shaking and shaking. I try, but I can't stay on the cloud.

"Mom, stop!" Deanna jumps up and grabs for Mom's wrists.

"Cut this out!" Mom shouts. She shoves Deanna away with her shoulder. "Do you hear me? You're punishing everybody!"

I flop around like a rag doll. Stella runs from her corner, papers flying everywhere.

"Stop that!" She breaks Mom's hold on my shoulders. My neck hurts. "You can't do that here."

"Don't you see?" Mom's tight fists push knuckle to knuckle against each other in her lap, and she looks up angrily at Stella. "It's an act. Always, it's an act. She only wants attention. If you give it to her, she'll only get worse."

Stella gazes calmly at Mom.

"Everyone in the whole world needs attention." Stella's words are slow and quiet, echoing like thunder through my brain.

"Huh!" Mom and Stella stare at each other. "She's my daughter. I know what she needs."

Two men in gray uniforms appear on either side of Stella. Mom shifts her twitching gaze to them and stands up.

"Don't worry," she says. "We're leaving."

She stalks to the door.

"Come on, Dee." She leaves without waiting for Deanna. She doesn't say good-bye to me or even look at me. I guess she's too upset. She'll remember next time. I really wish she'd kiss me good-bye, though. My cheek burns where she doesn't kiss me.

Deanna looks at me.

"You're so far away, Suzie," she says. "We can't stand it." She bends down and hugs me quick.

"Get better," she says, before running after Mom.

Wait! I wish I could call to her. *Don't leave me here!* But the door is swinging after her, and the words won't come anyway.

They've left me here again. I can't run after them. My legs don't work.

The pain of solid, uncried tears spreads from my chest through my whole body. All of my joints and bones hurt.

"You okay, Suzie?" Stella gazes down at me. "Did she hurt you?"

She watches me a few seconds, then moves slowly to the door, talking with the two men. Before I find my cloud, I hear Stella say, "We'll call you next time she visits. We didn't know."

I want to explain that Mom was just upset, that she thought if she shook me I'd start talking. That it always upsets her when I don't cooperate. It doesn't mean anything. Anybody's mom would be like that. She didn't hurt me. She'd never hurt me.

I wish I could talk. I wish I could cooperate. I feel so bad.

I concentrate real hard on my cloud. When it's around me, soft and gentle as a baby blanket, the pain fades away to almost nothing.

Almost.

❋❋❋

It's late and I'm lying in bed, waiting for Jody to come
with the IV. I'm not eating much yet, just a little apple
sauce today and yesterday. Looked at the ice cream. Maybe
tomorrow I'll try it. But the IV—I need the IV. I can't sleep
without it. My mind races and races, like a runaway train.
I work to slow down my thoughts, think logically, slowly,
in some kind of order.

Why am I here?

I know Mom doesn't want me here. She said so right at
the beginning. So why am I? Can't she take me home? Can't
parents just do stuff like that?

I don't get it. Why does she say I'm playing a game? What
does she mean about an act, about punishing? I'm not
doing anything like that. Not on purpose. I'm just being
who I am, doing what I do. I'm not trying to hurt or punish
anyone. How can what I do look like that?

What does she mean?

Here's what I do. I sit in a chair. That's my job—to sit
quietly and not bother anyone. I did it fine most of the time
at home. No one said I was punishing them. Why is Mom
saying it now? Nothing's different, except I'm at St.
Dorothy's.

I know there must be a reason I'm here. They wouldn't
keep me if they thought I was fine. Not being able to walk
right must be part of what's not fine. Crying, too, I guess.
And they want me to talk.

Talking! I'm sick of it. I wish people would stop trying to make me do it. That's the worst thing about being here. No matter where I am, no matter who I see, people push at me to talk. Talk talk talk. They just don't give up. Talk talk talk.

If they would only forget about it and leave me alone, I would be fine.

A car light from outside pulls the shadows in my room into odd shapes. The car moves on, and the shadows jump back into place.

Over the pillow, my brain shifts with a rising tide inside my head. I can't keep order there any more than I could hold those shadows. All the talking from everyone at St. Dorothy's combines and rises into a spiral, like an upside-down tornado. I can't understand any of the words, they're all so jumbled and red-angry. The noise rises higher and higher, shrieking like a hundred abandoned teakettles. AWFUL!

Wait. Stop. It's quiet here. No noise. No words. Slow down, brain.

I can't help it. The voices rise and crowd me until I remember again. It's noise in my head. Each time it starts up, I think NO! My NO! beats the wave of sound down to an angry calm, waiting for me to relax so it can start again.

"Ah, Suzie, you still awake?" Jody enters in the half light. "Got your IV ready."

Sleep. Sweet, sweet sleep.

Sunlight filters in between the threads of the see-through curtains on Stella's office windows, throwing greenish patches on the floor and on Stella's desk.

Stella's at her desk, a folder open in front of her, a pen lying across the papers. "Your mother lost her temper with you yesterday."

I'm not listening.

I sit on a green cloth chair and hug my knees while a soft breeze moves the curtains just enough. Just enough.

"Does your mom often hit you or shake you like that?"

Concentrate on those curtains. The breeze and the curtains are everything.

Stella leans across her desk toward me. "Do you think that's okay? Do you think your mom has a right to hurt you?"

Leave me alone. I don't want to hear this. Go away.

Stella sighs.

"Suzie, someone from the Child Welfare Department went to visit her this morning."

Child Welfare! They're the people who took the Simmons kids out of school last year because their mother wouldn't feed them. She only gave them cat food twice a week. At least that's what people said.

I feel angry. My mother isn't like that. She *cares* about me. Why are they bothering her?

"I have to report certain things to the authorities."

What things? She was just shaking me. I made her mad. Everyone's mom gets upset sometimes.

The curtains lift a little, and I feel that breeze. Mmmm. Warm August air. I let it wrap around me like my cloud, only green. Green and warm, warm and green.

"Suzie. Your face is blank. Where did you go?"

The softness drops away and I'm just here, where everything is ugly and cold.

Mom's visiting me in the solarium again. She's by herself this time, wearing her maroon business suit, and she's crocheting something green and white. Her maroon nail polish flashes through the fluffy yarn.

Stella said the Child Welfare people talked to Mom, but she's not saying that. She's talking about how the Coopers next door decided to move. They have a big orange cat named Tiger. Tiger's neat, the way he likes to stretch in the warm sun or the way he jumps into your lap and starts to purr. I guess I won't see him again. That makes me sadder. I feel tears behind my eyes, but I push them back. I don't want to upset Mom. I'm just so glad to see her.

"When you come home," she says, "I'll take you shopping. We'll buy you some nice clothes. Would you like that? Maybe a couple of blouses you can wear to school, and some jeans."

Clothes just for me? Not handed down from Deanna?

Mom smiles at me over her crocheting. I feel warm in that smile. See? She's a good person, not like Stella thinks. I made her lose her temper. Any mom could lose her temper.

"Someday," she's saying, "you'll have boyfriends like Deanna has. You'll want to look nice for them."

I like Tony, Deanna's boyfriend. He always tells knock-knock jokes. Some of them he makes up, like:

Knock knock.

Who's there?

Meet.

Meet who?

Meet me under the mistletoe and you'll find out.

I heard him say that to Deanna, and it was July. She laughed and kissed him anyway.

"This is so upsetting," Mom says.

Oh, no. It's my fault. Quick! What can I do? I concentrate on being silent, wrap my arms tighter around my legs, tighter, tighter. Will it be enough? I hold my breath and count while the bad stuff passes across Mom's face.

One second. Going. *Two seconds—*

Karen hops into the room in a half-squat. *Oh, no.* She stops to scratch her sides like an ape, snorting and going "Hoo-hoo, hoo-hoo."

Mom rubs her twitching eye and pulls out some stitches by mistake. She drops her crochet hook. Its clank on the floor draws Karen's attention to us.

"Hoo-hoo, hoo-hoo!" Snort, snort. She stares straight at Mom.

"Oh, this is awful!" Mom grabs her things and runs out of the room, past a man in a gray uniform. A security guard.

She never kissed me. Not once.

"Hoo-hoo, hoo-hoo," sings Karen. She hops over to my table. "You'll never get out of here," she says.

Hating Karen, I watch the swinging door, wishing I was anywhere else.

＊＊＊

Stella and I are in the solarium with a tray of hamburgers and milkshakes. I'm not eating my hamburger, but the milkshake goes down like a vanilla dream. I'm hardly even choking.

Stella has a piece of paper and a pencil.

"I know you're not talking," Stella says. "How about some writing?"

Writing. That's the same as talking, only quieter. You need words, and I don't have any.

Stella writes on the paper, "I have a dog named George. Do you have a pet?"

A pet?

Stella draws a picture of George. He's big and has shaggy fur. His collar has a heart on it. Stella writes "I love George" on the heart.

Then she puts a pencil in my hand.

"Write something," she says.

I look at the pencil, yellow against my skin. They're almost the same color. I'm yellow? Does that mean I'm a coward? I push the pencil against my finger, making the yellow almost white, then kind of pink. I'm not a coward.

"Suzie?" Stella's voice brings me back. Oh, yeah. Writing. Writing is talking. I cannot talk.

I look at Stella's words, "I love George." They're nice words. Stella's nice. Maybe if I copy her words, she'll like that. I don't know if I can, but they're in front of me.

They're her words, not mine. How did she write them, though? How did I used to do it? When I think about it, the letters fly in all directions like scattering piano keys. I see nothing but a white blank in my head and on the paper. How come I can read if I cannot write?

Stella sits back, drinking her milkshake like she has all the time in the world, like I'm the best company there is. I know I'm not.

Stella smiles at me. "Maybe," she says, "we'll take a walk tomorrow. There's a pond in the back where there are ducklings."

Ducklings. Soft, fuzzy, cute.

I look away and drop the pencil. It clatters on the table and rolls to the floor.

❋❋❋

When I was little, we had a Siamese cat named Sing Lo. The first time it snowed every year, he'd meow in his bass voice to go out the front door. He'd see the snow, maybe set one foot into it, then run back inside. He'd meow to go out the back door, then the side door. Just because it snowed in one place didn't mean there was snow every place. You could tell that's what he thought.

From year to year, he never gave up.

Sing Lo would eventually go outside. In this part of Pennsylvania, it hardly ever snows more than a little bit, and after a while he always figured out how to walk through it.

But the snow at my doors is high and deep and scary. There is no way out, except on my cloud.

✳✳✳

Stella and I are sitting by the duck pond. There's a mama duck walking all around, all around, like she doesn't know there are five little fuzzy creatures stumbling after her all the time. Three of them are yellow, two are black. Shouldn't they all be the same color? But they're not.

The mama brings them down to the water. Is this their first swim? They're so tiny. Have they tried it before? Will they know what to do?

The mama changes her mind. She climbs up the bank, walking all around the brushy ridge. None of the ducklings jump in, anyway. Even though they're only inches from the water, they don't disobey. They follow her, crowding each other and her. She acts like she's not even thinking about them. They don't ever forget where she is, though. They know that every second.

The mama walks right up to the edge of the ridge. Oh, no! She jumps, flapping her wings to land eight feet down on the water.

I'm almost afraid to watch the ducklings. Will they jump, too? Can their little wings carry them yet? But they don't try it. Instead, they turn around excitedly, running as fast as they can, following some secret diagonal path to the water. They trip over their feet and over each other in their rush to get wet. Two of the ducklings, one yellow, one black, fall down a little chute, somersaulting clumsily until they disappear in the vines.

I hold my breath. Will they be all right?

One by one, the ducklings find the water. I count the swimming ducklings—three yellows and one black. Where is the other one? I look at the mama. She doesn't look worried. I watch the shore. Out stumbles the fifth duckling from the greenery. He runs the rest of the way, like he can't wait, it's so much fun. They're all together.

"You have a lovely smile," says Stella.

I bite my lip, waiting for her to catch me at something, but she says nothing more.

＊＊＊

Margo from school is here.

Mom always said she's not much, not very smart, but she gets more A's than I do. I haven't seen her since she stopped by that one day in early summer—her or anybody else from school. But she's here. How does she know this is where I am?

We sit outside on the bench, under the weeping willow tree. The sun is warm on my skin. The bench is hard, green-painted wood under my rear end. Some of the paint is peeling, and I see black underneath.

Stella sits on another bench across the courtyard. Margo and I could have a private conversation if we wanted, but it doesn't matter. I'm not talking. I'm never going to talk. Don't they know this yet?

"We went to the beach over Labor Day," Margo says. "Dad bought us all popsicles from one of those pushcarts right on the sand. Mine was red. It was so hot the popsicles melted all over us before we could eat them. We ran into the water to wash off the sticky stuff, but there was a jellyfish that stung Tad, and he wouldn't go back into the water after that. I did, but I looked for that jellyfish."

I'm staring up at the sky, where the clouds are moving. I wish I was sitting on one. I've been having trouble finding my own cloud. Is it up there?

Margo turns my head with her hands, so I have to look into her gray eyes.

"Can you hear any of this?" she asks. "We miss you, Dale and Maureen and I. When are you coming back?"

I don't mean to, but I start crying. Margo puts her arms around me.

"You hear," she whispers. "You hear."

At first, I kept waking up every hour. That's how the spring began. Then it took me an hour to get to sleep, lying there staring at the dark ceiling. Later, it took me two hours, then three hours. I began to hate lying in my bed, tired and awake. I just couldn't relax.

"What's wrong with you?" Deanna asked me one morning in April. "Your hair's in your cereal."

I sat up better and brushed my soggy hair to the side. Great. Milky hair.

"I'm tired," I said. "I never can get to sleep until two or three."

Deanna glanced at Mom.

"Oh," said Mom. "That's a stage some girls go through."

Dad looked over his paper at Mom.

"It is!" she said, and he went back to his reading.

"I never did that," said Deanna.

"Lucky you," I said. "I hope this stage is over soon. I'm dragging all over the place."

I finished my breakfast and went off to school.

That day at lunch, I was hanging around as usual with Maureen, Dale, and Margo. Bonnie, a new kid from the Bronx, was sitting with us. Margo kept turning her head to speak to Bonnie, and I couldn't catch everything she said.

"Huh?" I asked for the fifth time. Margo rolled her eyes at me.

"Are you getting deaf?" Without waiting for an answer, she turned back to the others.

I knew Margo was trying to be funny, but she hurt my feelings. If I hadn't been so tired, I would have said right back, "No, but you're getting weird," or something that was part of our usual back-and-forth. But I didn't. I didn't have the energy. I did notice Margo looking back at me after a couple of seconds, like she wondered why I hadn't answered. I shrugged to myself. It was okay.

But I was too tired to try to listen anymore. This not-sleeping business was really getting to me. I slouched back in my seat and stared at the ceiling, feeling left out. Maybe Mom was right. Maybe Margo wasn't so much. Right now, she sure wasn't being great, with her back to me and her head bobbing at every word Bonnie said.

Oh, I didn't care. Let them talk. I gathered those pink pieces of cloud together like I'd been doing lately. Then I spiraled them around me until I was completely surrounded.

Ahh . . . weightlessness . . . higher and higher I went . . . it felt so good. Now I could relax.

"Hey!" Margo pushed my arm, banging my elbow on the table.

I crashed down from the cloud.

"Why'd you do that?" I rubbed my elbow.

"Didn't you hear the bell? Come on." She ran to catch up with the other girls waiting at the cafeteria door. I followed. I couldn't make myself hurry, even though I knew I'd be late. Each step was a struggle through thick molasses.

I *was* late. Mr. Barton stood at the door, watching me slog down the hall ten seconds after the bell.

"You walk like my grandmother," he said. "I should be telling you not to run, not telling you to speed up. But speed up."

I tried, but I couldn't make my legs move any faster.

Mr. Barton stopped me at the door. I looked up at him through my too-long bangs.

"You sick?" he asked. "Want to see the nurse?"

I shook my head. "Just tired," I said. Then I went to my seat and flopped down in it.

*** *** ***

It's nice out here today, with just the taste of fall in the air. Perfect for folding up inside my cloud. Cool and pink and fine. So fine.

"Karen?"

Uhhhh. Just the name makes me slide out of my cloud.

Jody's standing at the front door, shielding her eyes against the sun. "Karen?" she calls again. "Karen? Your parents are waiting for you."

Karen's not here. I'm glad. I can't sit and be still with her acting like a plane crash all the time. She likes to run into people, zigzagging around with her arms straight out. Three she got yesterday, screaming like a jet engine as she careened around the courtyard.

"EeeyoooEeeeeyoooEee . . ." All while wearing a dress. She always wears a worn-out dress. Yesterday's had a velvet strip half torn from the waistline, showing the plain brownish material underneath.

She was heading for me when Bill stopped her.

Now Jody runs down the steps. "Wasn't Karen out here, Bill?"

"She's . . ." Bill pulls his attention from a game of tag to make a quick search with his eyes. "Oh, no. She was reading on the steps, but . . ." He sprints for the gate. That doesn't make sense, though. There's a guard there. How could she get out?

Suddenly, the rest of us have to go inside. I don't know

why, but Jody and the other grown-ups are gathering us together. Why, though? We're not the ones missing. We didn't do anything wrong.

I'm so slow, even with Jody helping me. Everyone else is up the steps and inside, and we're still on the grass. Each leaf of the rhododendrons trembles in the breeze, laughing at me.

Slowpoke, slowpoke, slowpoke.

The rhododendrons are mean. So mean the leaves even form to make a mean face. Wait. That's Karen's face, looking out with those narrowed eyes.

Karen's hiding in the rhododendrons. Why?

She sees me looking at her, and her eyes get even narrower. She tells me through those evil slits, "You better not tell, you better not tell."

My eyes are on Karen when I trip on the bottom step. Jody loses her grip on my elbow as I fall.

Hhhh! Hurts, hurts. Hhhh! Ow, ow, ow, ow!

Jody helps me up.

"Oh, Suzie," says Jody. "I'm sorry. Oh, look at your knees!"

Bleeding. Both of them.

It's Karen's fault.

Jody helps me up the steps. Karen is the last one outside, and I'm the only one who knows it.

"I got a call from one of your teachers," said Mom. "Mrs. Spence. She says you fell asleep in her class three times this week."

"She's boring," I said. "And I'm tired all the time. I can't wait for this stage to be over. I can never sleep at night."

Mom put down the paper she was holding.

"Look, Suzie," she said. "You can't fall asleep in class just because some teacher is boring."

"Well, she is. She makes history sound like soggy bread. Yucky. Who wants to listen to that, anyway?"

"She says you don't comb your hair anymore. She thinks you might be depressed."

I touched my hair. Dirty, too. I didn't care.

"You have to comb your hair, Suzie. You have to be presentable."

"I'm just so tired all the time," I said.

"I know. But you have to make the effort, or teachers begin to be upset."

I sat on the couch, holding a corduroy throw pillow against my stomach. I didn't care if the teachers were upset. I just cared that I couldn't sleep.

"What did you tell Mrs. Spence?" I asked.

"I told her you were going through a stage. We hoped you'd be through it soon."

I tried harder after that. I washed and combed my hair. And I never fell asleep in Mrs. Spence's class after that.

But one day in Mr. Barton's, I did.

Margo was shaking my shoulder. I woke up and saw Mr. Barton's face above Margo's. The whole class was staring at me, laughing.

"You with us now, Suzie?" he asked. Then he went back to the blackboard.

But the other kids kept looking back and laughing.

I went home by myself that afternoon. I didn't want to talk to anyone. I just wanted to go home and look for my cloud. Anymore, that's what got me through the day— remembering that I could roll up in my cloud after school. Rising high and higher. Look, there's dark little Suzie in her dark little box. But I'm up here, drifting and drifting.

It was the cloud that pulled me home, that kept me from sitting on the curb or sitting down just anywhere. Once I was there, I could safely sit in my cloud as long as I needed.

But just inside the door . . .

Smack!

Right across the face.

"I told you about sleeping in school!"

Smack!

"Mom! Stop!" I crouched on the floor, covering my face with my hands. My backpack took a lot of the blows, but not all. My face stung from the old sores, and my hands hurt, too.

"I don't need these teachers calling here all the time."

"But I didn't mean to . . ."

"Doesn't matter what you mean. It's what you do. Now you go upstairs to your room, and you think about this."

A blow to the ear. "Maybe it will help you stay awake in school."

"Corynne!"

I lifted my head. Dad was there in the dining room doorway, still holding his briefcase. He must have just come in through the garage. Deanna was on the steps. Both of them were staring at Mom and me.

"What are you doing, Corynne? Why are you hitting Suzie like that?"

"She's my daughter," Mom said. Her eye twitching, she walked up to Dad with her right fist raised, like she might hit him. Sometimes she did. "I was punishing her. Do you have something to say?" She closed the distance between them until he backed away.

Behind him, I saw an open wine bottle on the dining room table. In a minute, he'd see it, too.

"No, no." Then, "You've been drinking. I smell it."

I stayed on my knees until I got to the stairs. Then, staying low, I crept up silently after Deanna.

"So what?" was Mom's reply. I heard the scuff of the bottle as she grabbed it off the table.

When we got to my room, I closed the door and flopped sideways onto the bed. We could hear Mom and Dad arguing in the kitchen. Normal stuff.

My backpack was still on my back, pulling against my shoulders, but I didn't care. I was too tired to move.

Deanna asked, "Are you all right?"

"It's my hands. I wish she'd stay away from my hands."

Deanna gave me the lotion from my bureau. I sat up and

slathered it on. Some of the sore feeling dropped away, but not all of it. I let my backpack fall onto the floor.

"I've got to figure out how to stay awake in school," I said. "I wish I could sleep at night."

"Summer vacation's coming," said Deanna. "You'll get it straightened out by then."

"Think so?"

"Sure. It's just a stage, right? That means it won't last."

"I hope *I* last," I said.

That night, I stayed awake all night. I stared at the ceiling for the first hour. Then I sat up at the window, watching the red brake lights come on as cars slowed before the stop sign at the end of the street.

I went down to breakfast as usual. Without any sleep at all, I felt like I was moving under water. But I was awake.

"Why are you sitting like that?" asked Deanna.

I looked down at myself. My feet were on the chair, and my knees were up at my chest. I put my feet on the floor.

"You look like you're about to pass out," Deanna said.

"Tired," I said. "No sleep."

Deanna shook her head, then looked sideways at Mom by the coffeemaker. Dad was reading the paper. Neither one was really paying attention. Regular morning stuff.

"Mom and Dad, look at Suzie."

I gave Deanna a *NO* look, but it was too late.

Dad folded down his paper to look at me. Mom turned away from the coffeemaker, stirring her mug's worth with a spoon. Her eyes were on me, too.

I started to cry. I didn't mean to, and I don't know why it

happened. But the tears rolled down my cheeks.

"Oh, Lord," said Mom. She put her coffee down.

"What's wrong, Suzie?" asked Dad.

"Nothing," I said. But then I started sobbing.

Deanna put her hand on mine. "Suzie needs a day at home. She isn't feeling well. Probably your period, right?"

I didn't have my period yet. Deanna knew that.

Mom started pacing up and down.

"Are you going to stay home with her, Deanna?" she asked. "I have a full schedule today. And Dad's leaving for Tucson this morning."

"I'll stay home with her," said Deanna. "I don't mind."

Mom stopped and drank from her mug before she started pacing again, faster this time. I knew what Mom was going to do. I had to stop my crying jag before she did it.

I pushed my napkin against my forehead as hard as I could. I forced the tears to stop. It was hard, but I had to do it. There. Done.

"It's okay," I said. One more silent sob rocked my body, but Mom was facing the other way. "I'm fine now."

I shook off Deanna's hand and put my breakfast dishes in the dishwasher. Deanna chased me up the steps.

"How are you going to get through the day?" she asked.

"I don't know," I said, "but Mom was going to hit me again. I couldn't take another one."

Deanna looked down at me from her sixteen years. "I'll tell you what I think," she said. "I think Mom's the one going through a stage."

I picked up my homework and stuffed it into my

backpack. "She still feels bad about February," I said. "She thinks I'm trying to punish her when I cry."

"Are you?"

"No. I just feel awful. How'd you like to get no sleep for a couple of centuries?"

Deanna looked out my room toward the stairs. Mom's voice was rising in anger above Dad's.

"You're a good-for-nothing with a good-for-nothing job," we heard. "Any other woman would have thrown you out years ago."

Crash!

"It pays the mortgage on this house!"

"I don't know why you have to work for a brother who pays you beans!"

Crash!

"Come on," said Deanna. "While they're still in the kitchen."

I grabbed my half-zipped backpack. She grabbed her red one from behind her bedroom door, and we raced down the stairs and out the door. We didn't stop running until the intersection. For some reason, we were laughing when we stopped. It felt so good to laugh. We sat down on the curb and laughed and laughed.

"Why are we laughing?" I asked.

"I don't know."

We laughed some more. Then, instead of carrying our backpacks in our hands, we put them over our shoulders. We kept on down the street, laughing every now and then. Then I stopped. "Lunch," I said. "We forgot our lunches."

Deanna dug into her jeans. "We're not going back for them. Here."

I didn't take the two dollars at first. I knew it was baby-sitting money. But she pushed it at me.

"I'll pay you back," I said.

Deanna smiled at me. Then she started laughing again. So did I.

After we'd gone a couple more blocks, a turquoise van passed us.

"There goes Dad," Deanna said. "On his way to Tucson."

"I guess he didn't see us," I said. "He didn't wave."

We walked on without talking or laughing for another minute.

"I know what," said Deanna. "When you come home this afternoon, come in the back door and go straight up to your room. Just in case. I'll warn you if Mom's not okay."

More silence. Then we broke out into laughter again. Gales of it, until Deanna left me at the middle school . . .

. . . Later, the laughter was long gone, and I was so tired.

"I'm eating by myself today," I told Margo on the way to the lunchroom.

"Why?"

"I just am." No energy for explanations.

Margo looked hurt. "Are you mad at us?"

I shook my head. "Just tired."

I took a corner table. I wasn't hungry because I was so tired, so I didn't use Deanna's money after all. I put my head down, and in what felt like a minute, I woke up to people's feet tramping past me. Lunchtime was over, and my thirty minutes of sleep were just enough to get me through the day . . .

. . . Deanna was sitting on the porch steps eating an orange popsicle when I got home.

"Mom's shopping," she told me. "It's just us at home."

I nodded and went inside and up to my room.

"I'll tell you when I see her car," Deanna called up the stairs after me.

"Thanks."

I collapsed on my bed. Safe for awhile.

There's Edgar again. He keeps trying to get me to draw. Doesn't he know that drawing is talking? If I could talk, I know he wouldn't care if I drew a thing. Ever. I sit, holding the fat black crayon that he puts in my hand.

Joshua, a boy about my age, sits next to me. He's drawing a picture of a fire. Big orange flames shoot out in every direction. They crowd me, and I can't get my breath. I close my eyes, trying not to see.

"Look, Suzie, look," he says. "A campfire. Marshmallows."

I jump up, knocking my chair back. Something . . . something . . .

Joshua looks up at me, his mouth open, his eyes wide, still holding the orange crayon. Edgar grabs me so I don't fall. Stella runs over from the doorway.

"What is it, Suzie?" she asks. "What is it?"

It's— It's— The scream rising from my gut becomes ash before it forms and falls to nothing. Nothing.

Embarrassed, I sit down again. It's just a picture. A picture. Crayons and paper, that's all.

Joshua gives me a long stare, then goes back to drawing.

"A campfire," he continues. He's not talking to me, but to the empty chair on the other side. "Last July. It was last July, remember, Ray? I told you. The day after we heard the rattler."

Ray? But nobody's there.

*** *** ***

Dad's here today. It's raining outside, so we're in the solarium. He's wearing a suit with that floppy red bow tie he calls his clown tie. He's sitting where Mom was the last time I saw her. I wonder why Mom isn't here, too.

"I've been away," Dad says. "I sent you some cards. Did you get them?"

One was blue with a green and gold butterfly on the front.

"Uncle Elliot's got me going all over, troubleshooting his new stores. But I think about you all the time. I'm going to Dallas tomorrow and Houston next week. I wish I could stay here and see you."

He never stayed home and saw me before. He thinks about me all the time? Did he ever think about me before? I couldn't tell. Why now? I feel like he's lying, but I don't know why.

Uncle Elliot's making him visit you. It's my mother's voice inside my head. But I think it's true. Dad and I live in the same house, but he never noticed me much. Not that he was mean. He just didn't see me.

We stare at the rain. The wind pushes the weeping willow all over the place.

"It's a tropical storm," says Dad. "It was called Bertha when it was a hurricane. It rearranged the Carolina coast."

This visit is strange. Dad's telling me this because he doesn't know what else to say. He doesn't know what to say,

55

and I can't say anything. Some conversation.

Dad shifts in his chair and sighs a deep sigh. He feels bad about me.

"Margo says you can hear. How can I tell? You just sit there like a statue. You don't even move. They say you're eating better. Why don't you speak? If you would only speak . . ." His voice trails away.

I have no words. How can I speak if I have no words?

Dad leaves, but first he kisses me on the cheek.

"I love you."

My chest hurts, like I was hit with a baseball. I can hardly breathe. But I stay still, holding it all in.

*** *** ***

I'm sitting in a circle with a bunch of other people. Group therapy is what they call it. I guess someone thinks I'll forget and talk to a bunch of strangers. I don't care. I don't have anything to say, anyway. I can sit here same as anywhere else. They talk, I don't listen. I've got too much stuff in my own head to think about someone else's problems.

For instance, I am eating better now. Sometimes I'm even hungry. And I don't choke much. So no more IVs. I don't like IVs. It's hard to put my arms around my knees with that tube in the way.

I can swallow the pills, too. That's important. Happy pills, Karen calls the ones we get at breakfast. How can she say that with her face so mad all the time? But the pills don't make me happy, either. I don't feel any different at all, but Stella says I will. How can pills make you happy?

The sleeping pills are the important ones. With them, my brain can slow down and I can sleep. I like sleep. Sleep, sleep, sleep. I wish I could take more pills so I could sleep all the time. Being awake stinks. Everything is gravel-gray damp. I sit here. I sit there. It doesn't matter where. Not much matters. Even the sunshine is gray.

Nobody else in this room needed help walking here. I don't know why I can't get my legs to work better. Jody tells me it'll happen. I guess she knows.

"You're a basketball player." Jody was walking me down

the hall behind everyone else. "I can see that with your long legs."

Basketball players run. I can't even walk.

All day long, people try to get me to talk. It makes me mad. Can't they figure it out? I can't talk. They think I could if I would try, but I can't. *Can't!* I don't have any words. I don't think I even like words. People use them, say anything they feel like saying.

Some words hurt like fire. People say them anyway, like they don't notice. Or care. Besides, how can I find my cloud with people jabbering at me all the time?

So I sit quietly and still, taking up as little room as possible, until they give up and go away. Eventually, everybody does. At least for awhile.

The room is suddenly quiet. The people are all looking at me. It's my turn to talk. That's stupid. I don't talk. What do they think is going to happen, that I'll stand up and sing? I don't like everyone looking at me, either. It's not fair, making me come in here, trying to force me to talk, letting everyone stare at me when I don't. It's mean. Karen laughs. So do the others, but she starts it. Her laugh is as mean as her face.

I stiffen, staring at the green-painted wall over the heads opposite me. Concentrating, concentrating. I lift myself to my living room at home. Gold carpet, gold curtains, gold wallpaper, golden chair, the anniversary clock's golden weight revolving on the mantle. Me sitting there quiet. Everything in its place. I'm there.

"You're a stone." Karen's voice cuts through to where I

am. "Stone, stone, stone." The last three words are high and scratchy. "Stone, stone, stone."

"That's enough, Karen," says Stella.

Jody helps me to my feet. Group therapy must be over. Good. Until next time.

"Come on, Suzie," she says. "Don't you listen to that. I know you're not a stone."

We walk behind the rest of the group at our slow pace. Karen turns around. Her grin turns her face into a Halloween mask. Scary.

"Stone, stone, stone," she shouts at me one last time before running down the hall, her skirt flying behind her.

Am I a stone? Almost. But my heart beats. That must count for something.

※※*※*

Joshua's working on a jigsaw puzzle next to the solarium's big window. I watch him from my chair. I don't know why he's at St. Dorothy's. He seems all right to me. He talks, anyway. That seems to be the most important thing around here. Sometimes he talks to people who aren't there, but at least he talks. He has words. How does he have words?

Right now, he's talking to me.

"I'm sorry if my picture scared you the other day," he says.

But it didn't. Not really. Who'd be scared of crayons?

He picks up a blue border piece and finds the right place for it. He looks at another, then drops it for a different one. He fits that one into place. How does he see where each piece fits? They all look the same to me.

"It wasn't supposed to be a scary picture. Just a campfire with my dad and me roasting marshmallows. We used to go camping, just my dad and me. We'd sit around the campfire at night, drinking hot cider and singing silly songs."

He sings, "My gal's a corker, she's a New Yorker / I buy her everything to keep her in style / She's got a pair of hips just like two battleships / Hey, boys, that's where my money goes." He holds the last word long so it goes up and down. "See? That kind of stuff."

He fits in another puzzle piece.

"I'd like to go camping with my dad again."

Do people really do that? Go camping and sing silly

songs? I don't believe in it. But the silly song is real. Can you have the silly song without the campfire and the marshmallows?

"I can't, though. That's what my mother says."

Joshua looks at me.

"My dad went away. He's coming back. I know he is."

Joshua's face gets all red. I think he will split in two.

Without thinking, I put my hand on his shoulder. Joshua's eyes get round like quarters. He looks at me like I'm a ghost.

✳✳✳

"Mom, remember that day in February?" I was sitting on the gold-upholstered chair in the living room. My favorite place to sit.

"I thought we weren't going to talk about that anymore." Mom looked up from painting varnish on a chair, newspapers spread out like a fan around her. Anger flashed across her face and disappeared. "That's history."

"I know." I was on thin ice, but something made me go on. "But I think . . ." I watched her face to gauge her reaction to my words. "I think that might be . . . why I'm so tired all the time."

"No." She shook her head and went back to the varnishing. "It's a stage."

"But Mom—"

"It's a stage you'll outgrow." She was very definite.

"I don't think so. And I can't stop thinking about that day. And . . ." Now I could hear my voice rising.

"Suzie, you're hurting my feelings by bringing this up. Now, cooperate and stop talking. You'll get yourself all wound up, me upset, and then I'll have to do something." She stopped varnishing to look at me. I knew what she meant.

My ears began to ring. I swallowed a couple of times, but that didn't fix it. Was I catching a cold?

"Besides," she went on, "that day is over. Done. No reason to think about it unless you want to make me feel bad. You're succeeding, if that's what you're after."

I didn't want her to feel bad, so I stopped talking. I guessed she was right. I was going through a stage. I wanted to believe that. Pretty soon, I'd be sleeping every night. Oh, I wanted that so much.

Mom kept working. The ringing in my ears went away, and I felt better. No cold.

Deanna asked me later if I wanted the first shower. Mom was watching, so I didn't answer. I knew once I opened my mouth, I'd have trouble not talking about February. It was all I could think of. So I didn't answer. That was the safest way. When I didn't answer, Mom looked relieved and shook her head.

"You take the first shower, Dee," Mom said. "Suzie's onto a no-talking act."

"Huh?"

Mom gestured to Dee not to ask anymore.

"Why isn't Suzie talking?" Deanna asked Mom in the kitchen a few minutes later. I guessed they thought I couldn't hear them from my golden chair. "And she's sitting in that funny way again."

"Suzie's strange," said Mom. "Leave her alone."

But when Deanna came out of the kitchen, she offered me a cookie.

"You must be hungry," she said. "You aren't eating much lately."

I didn't like cookies, so I shook my head.

❋❋❋

Uncle Elliot and Aunt Olga visit me in the solarium.

Why are they here?

"We baked you some cookies," says Aunt Olga.

"Your favorite," puts in Uncle Elliot.

Aunt Olga places a wrapped plate on the table and pulls away the plastic. The wrinkled plastic is nightmare gray, and I don't like the look of the cookies with their chocolate eyes. I wish someone would take them away. Throw them away. Cookies!

"I'm sorry you're having such a bad time," says Uncle Elliot. "Are you feeling any better?"

Even if I had words, I don't know what I would say. Except for having to look at the cookies, I'm not having a bad time. They look like a nightmare with a fever. I lift my head so I can't see them. Feel better than what, anyway? I'm not crying, so what does he mean?

When I don't answer, Uncle Elliot raises his eyebrows at Aunt Olga.

She leans forward.

"Wouldn't you be more comfortable sitting with your fanny on the chair and your feet on the floor? That looks like about the hardest way to sit, the way you're doing it."

I'm not moving. This is the way I sit. What's the big deal?

Aunt Olga shrugs her tiny shoulders under her black and white check blouse.

Uncle Elliot tries again.

"Did you like the black-eyed Susan shirt we sent you?"

You gave me that? Why?

"Can we bring you anything else? Maybe some books or magazines? Tapes?" Uncle Elliot's voice gets higher and tighter as he talks. He sounds upset, but he must not be. There's nothing to be upset about. "Is there something we can do to help you?"

Here's what I want: to be left alone. I don't need anything. Except to go home.

Aunt Olga says, "We'd love to have you come visit us when you're okay. You can swim in our pool or play with our cats. I'll teach you how to make jam."

I can't do that stuff. Can't you see that? I sit. That's what I do.

And I'm okay right now. I'd be really okay if I was home. Other people think otherwise, but that's them. It's not fair that other people get to decide that I'm not okay. It's not fair that I have to be here because of what other people think. What was wrong with staying home in my chair? I wasn't hurting anyone, was I?

Uncle Elliot grasps my hands with his own.

"You're a special person," he says. "You're an eagle. Don't you remember that?"

I look at his hands, warm and huge and covered with dark hair. I feel the callouses under his fingers.

Why are Uncle Elliot and Aunt Olga here? Why does Uncle Elliot say I'm special? I'm not pretty like Deanna. I don't get A's in math like Margo. I just sit. That's not special. It's not even interesting. That's the point—so I can be left alone.

"Maybe short visits are best, El," says Aunt Olga. She pulls on his arm gently. "She needs time."

Uncle Elliot looks at me like he's got something on his mind. Like he's mad, but not at me.

"Did something happen?" he asks. "What was it?"

I've heard these questions before, but it makes me feel bad to hear them from Uncle Elliot. He's someone from before. The other people here don't know me. Not like that.

"You should have seen her, Olga, when she learned how to ride her bike. You should have seen her. You never saw anyone so thrilled, so lit up."

My bike. I see it, bent and cracked under the car. NO! Don't think of it!

"I know, El, I know." Aunt Olga speaks like he's told her that before. "She'll be happy again. You'll see."

I find my cloud, finally, and I go there. Peace. That's what I want.

There's a scraping of chairs, and my aunt and uncle stand up. Uncle Elliot's brow is creased, and Aunt Olga shakes her head. Her eyes are wide and dark. My cloud comes down a little ways, so I can kind of hear but don't have to come back.

"Did you see the way her face just went blank?" Aunt Olga asks. From my cloud, I see her wave her hand in front of my eyes. I don't even blink in that box of mine.

They stop to speak to Stella on their way out. More shaking of heads and serious voices.

What do they want? I don't get it. What do they really want?

❋❋❋

I stopped talking one day. I know that. What I don't know is why I stopped being *able* to talk. I mean, I stopped talking on purpose. That was right after school was out for the summer. All my talking was doing was getting me into trouble or hurting other people's feelings. So I stopped. But then my mother asked me a question one afternoon. It was a simple question.

"Where's Deanna?"

I couldn't find the words. I opened my mouth. I knew Deanna was outside, but I couldn't say it.

"What's the matter?" Mom asked.

My mouth was still open. I took one breath, then another. There were no words. I couldn't find any. I was so shocked, the tears just started.

"Oh, Lord." Mom turned away. "Well, you have a good cry," she said. "I'll find her."

Deanna walked in just then.

"What's wrong, Suzie?" she asked.

I wanted them to go away. I couldn't stop crying as long as they were there, and I knew Mom hated it when I cried.

"It's . . . never mind." Mom pulled Deanna out of the room. "We'll leave her alone." I could hear their voices in the kitchen, but I didn't even try to understand them.

Later, Deanna came back. I'd stopped crying by then. "Let me take you to your bed," she said. She took my hand and led me up the steps. "You're so tired you're about to drop. I'll read to you, like old times. Would you like that?"

She helped me into my bed, covered me with the sheet, and picked up *The Secret Garden*, the closest book on my shelf. Deanna read a long time, while I went back and forth from my cloud. While Mary Lennox traveled in the gray rain in that old-fashioned carriage, I finally fell gently asleep.

When I woke up, it was dark. Deanna was still there.

I sat up.

"Have a good sleep?" she asked.

I nodded. I would have thanked her for reading, but I couldn't find the words.

The next day, Dad was home. He didn't like it that I wasn't talking. He was gesturing at me on my golden chair.

"Corynne, how can this be a stage?" he demanded.

I was surprised he said anything about it. Usually, he just walked around me, thinking his own thoughts. Now he was circling me, pointing at me, pushing at me.

Cloud, cloud, where are you?

"Alex, you're not even here most of the time." Mom's voice was accusing. "What do you know about it? Suzie's got a problem, sure. And when she's ready to talk about it, we're here. Deanna and I are, anyway. You could be in Texas or North Dakota being an errand boy for good old Elliot. But I'm here. She's all right with me. I'm taking care of her while you dance around the country."

Dad was shaking his head.

"You'd be sitting on the curb without my job," he said.

"How much do music lessons pay?"

"You think I can't sing, either. Isn't that right?" Her hand was coming up.

Dad backed away. "Corynne, I never said that. I love your singing. Everyone does."

"I gave up my career for this family. Sacrificed my voice so I could take care of our daughters. And what do I get? An absent husband who thinks he has better answers when he decides to show up. Suzie'll be fine. You just leave her to me."

"But—" he said, and his voice was quiet now. "Look at her. She just sits there like she's got awful cramps. Why won't she talk?" He came to stand in front of me. "Why, Suzie? What's wrong?"

I couldn't have given him an answer if I'd had one. The words were gone for good. But it didn't matter.

He shrugged his shoulders and walked away.

"Okay, Corynne. I guess you know what's best. She's your job."

I'm in my cloud. Safe here. I wish I could always be here. Pinks dissolve and grow into blues, greens, and more blues. Beautiful and soft, like peacock feathers.

Bang! I crash to the floor. Karen's standing over me, holding my chair. I want to scream, but I can't get any air. Oh, no, oh, no! She's going to kill me!

She swings the chair, catching one of the legs on her hem. It tears as she smashes the chrome and plastic against the wall. There's a spark, and the chair lands sideways with one leg bent. I push along the floor, backing up, backing up. But I know I can't get away.

Karen turns to me, panting. What's she going to do? Her torn hem hangs down almost to her knees. I want to get up, but she won't let me.

"You're always sitting like you're asleep," she says. "Like you don't know what's happening around you." Wind from an open door somewhere blows her curls. "Stay awake!"

I shield my face with my hurting hands.

Karen kicks me sharply on the leg, then walks away, laughing. At the turn in the hall, she stops cackling and looks back, her mean look burning worse than the kick.

"Now stay awake!"

❋ ❋ ❋

I think about the day Uncle Elliot taught me how to ride my bike. Afterwards, we sat on the porch steps. I was still out of breath, so I didn't say much. He leaned his elbow on the top step and smiled down at me. Mom was still practicing.

Sometimes I feel . . .

"You're an eagle," he said.

"Yeah." I smiled back.

Flying down the street sure felt good. I was going to do it again as soon as the stitch in my side went away.

Like a motherless child . . .

"Eagles fly anywhere they want," Uncle Elliot said. "Remember that."

"Okay." I didn't know what he meant. Not really.

A long way from home . . .

Uncle Elliot stood up when Dad pulled his car into the driveway. Dad waved as he parked.

"Your mom's sounding pretty good. Her big concert's coming up, isn't it?"

"Yeah. She practices all the time, anymore. She says we'll go somewhere for ice cream afterwards."

A long way from home . . .

Then Uncle Elliot left to go somewhere with Dad.

In a minute, I got back on my bike.

Sometimes I feel . . .

"Like an eagle!" I shouted.

And I flew away from the house.

Stella has George with her. He's on a leash close to Stella's knee.

I'm so scared. Dogs bite! Blood, red and big, stains your shirt and drips onto the sidewalk. That's what happened to Deanna when Baron—a boxer—escaped from his fenced-in yard across the street.

Deanna was hurt! Deanna was hurt!

"It's okay!" Deanna shouted at me over my screaming.

I couldn't stand it. Deanna held me, dripping blood onto my shoulder. All that blood. Deanna's.

"Suzie, calm down! Baron's gone."

Deanna had five stitches next to her left breast. I had nightmares.

I can't make my mind blank with George right here, so big, so big. His whole body moves with each breath.

I wait for George's body to tense up before the pounce, wait for his teeth to sink into my skin.

"George is gentle," Stella says to Joshua and me. "You can pet him."

I sit so still. I'm scared, but I can't move. I can't even turn my head. Even moving can be talking.

Joshua leaves his seat as soon as he sees George.

"Hi, George," he says. He pets George's long smooth fur. "Good doggie, nice doggie." Joshua turns to look at me. "Are you afraid, Suzie? He's a good dog. He won't hurt you, will he, Stella?"

"No, indeed," says Stella.

My box comes in close. It makes me bring my feet up under my bottom. It comes closer still. There's hardly room to breathe. If I could only leave. I'm so scared. I look for my cloud and find it. Now I'm higher and safer in the warm pink light. So high I can't hear Stella and Joshua talking.

But I can see Joshua put his head on George's wide back. Joshua looks happy.

****

We went to Mom's concert in a big auditorium in New York. Not many people were there, and we knew most of them. Dad said that didn't matter, because Mom was just getting started. Uncle Elliot and Aunt Olga came, and so did all of Mom's voice students. There were some people I never saw before, but not many.

While Mom stood on the stage and sang, I closed my eyes and followed the songs I knew so well. Somehow, her voice reminded me of liquid rose-colored glass. It was even better than in our living room. Everybody liked it and clapped real hard at the end of each song. I clapped the hardest. Mom smiled up there and bowed in her long, turquoise dress with the glitter at the shoulders. It was wonderful.

That was what we said at the ice-cream place later. That's what we said all the way home. Mom was so excited she said she wished she could go back and do it again.

But at breakfast time the next morning, Mom was lying on the couch with a washcloth over her face. Deanna was huddled in one of the easy chairs under a blanket. Dad put his finger over his lips when he saw me.

"What happened?" I whispered.

"Bad reviews," Dad whispered back. "They said she sang out of tune and sounded like a train stopping."

Why did they say that? She never sounded like that.

"Mom, I'm sorry," I said.

I touched her arm.

"Get away from me!" she growled.

I jumped back and looked at Dad. He didn't say anything at first. Only sighed.

Then he said, "Leave her alone for awhile. That's what she wants."

I went into the kitchen and had the quietest breakfast I could. Then I walked to school, even though it was early, so Mom could have quiet. Deanna walked with me as far as the middle school.

"Some days," she said before going inside, "school comes in very handy."

When I came home that afternoon, a loud *skerrunk!* pulled me onto the grass next to the driveway.

Mom was there, driving the van over my bike.

What?

She kept running over it, backward and forward, backward and forward.

My bike, my bike. What was Mom thinking? Did she know what she was doing?

I waved my hands at her real fast. "Mom! Hey!"

Her face through the closed window was red and angry, almost on fire. Her lips moved while she stared straight ahead. She never looked at me. How could I stop her?

BANG-CLANK! A metal chunk flew away from the rest of the bike, almost hitting my shoulder. *Thunk.* It hit the ground behind me. Hardly thinking, I picked it up. It was hot! But I held onto it. I hugged the broken piece of handlebar against my chest and sobbed.

My bike was wrecked, but Mom kept driving over it. I could never ride it again. My beautiful bike. Lost. Gone.

But it was my bike, broken or not. It was important. I wanted it!

I ran toward the van, toward my mother. "Mom, stop. Stop!"

Deanna grabbed my arm before I got close. Where'd she come from? I looked at her. A red scratch ran down her cheek.

"Come on, Suzie," she shouted over the noise. "Let's get out of here. Mom's gone nuts."

"My bike . . ." I made a move toward it, but Deanna yanked me up the sidewalk.

"Forget it, Suzie."

Deanna let me pause to watch Mom make another pass over my bike. It shook violently before it disappeared underneath the van.

Between sobs, I asked, "Why is she wrecking my bike?"

"She's wrecking everything," Deanna said. "She threw the mantle clock at me when I came home. I've been waiting for you on the porch ever since." She pulled me up the sidewalk.

"But what did we do to her? Why's she blaming us?"

Deanna had no answer.

When we got to the next street, we turned into the neighborhood park. Children were playing on swings while their mothers watched. We kept on going down the hill until we were away from other people. Then we sat on a bench under a huge beech tree.

"We'll stay here for awhile," said Deanna. "Give her time to wear herself out. Or pass out." Deanna's voice sounded hard, bitter.

"What are we going to do?"

"We'll just stay out of her way for a few days. Then she'll be all right."

"What's happening?"

"You don't remember how she used to drink and throw things around, do you? That's what it is. She's drinking again. She couldn't take the reviews, Suzie, and she's drinking." She paused. "That's what it is."

I pushed circles into the palm of my hand with all that was left of my bike. Across the field, where daisies danced in the breeze, it all seemed so peaceful. Seemed.

Joshua kicks a soccer ball in the courtyard. He kicks it around the trees and bushes and back again. He stops in front of my bench.

"Play with me?" he asks. Then, when I don't move, he sits down next to me, holding the ball. "You're so afraid all the time. Why are you afraid?"

I'm not afraid. Why does he think so?

"It won't hurt to kick the soccer ball around," he says. "There's nothing to be afraid of. Honest."

He thinks I'm afraid to kick the soccer ball? I don't feel afraid, but I can't do it. It's not that I won't. Why can't I, though? I don't know. But I can't. What if I try? The thought makes me shiver. My heartbeat quickens. I half remember yelling and hard hits. I push away those thoughts. I can't look at them.

"No one will yell at you."

Yell at me? Yell? Why does he say that? What does he know? I don't want to think about this.

He takes my hand away from my face.

"Come on. I'll show you where there's a bunch of butterflies."

My body is stone. I do not move.

"No one will yell at you for walking across the courtyard." He points. "See? There's Stella. You'll be fine."

I look at Stella on her bench. My palms are sweating, my heart thumping.

Joshua sounds so serious, like he really means it. Does he mean it? Do people mean it? Is he going to yell? My face is hot, reliving scorn. I don't want to get hit.

I look at Stella again. She's smiling.

What if I do . . . ?

Slowly, I take my knees away from my chin to sit with my legs hanging down from the bench. I don't like the way it feels, without my legs up against my chest. I push myself to stand up, all the time watching Stella, watching Joshua. They're watching me. Are they waiting for me to do something wrong? So they can yell? Hit? I can't tell. I hold my cloud close, just in case, waiting for the scornful, stinging words. I walk two steps. They're hard steps. My legs are as heavy as concrete, but I take those steps. Alone.

Suddenly, I don't know what's happening. There's so much sound, and Joshua's jumping up and down like a crazy person. I freeze, panicked.

"It's okay," says Stella. She holds my hands, so I can't put them over my face. "Don't be afraid."

Together, we watch Joshua leap around us, doing war whoops.

"He's so happy for you," Stella says.

Happy? He's showing happy?

Leaping around and war whoops.

For me.

***

We have pineapple slices with lunch today. I don't like pineapples. Neither does Joshua. He never eats them.

Today I'm not eating them, either. Not eating them is talking. Nobody knows that. It's a secret.

Mashed potatoes look like mountains of paste on my plate. They don't taste much better. So I'm not eating them. I put my napkin over them, they're so ugly. No more mashed potatoes or pineapple slices. Ever again.

No one notices this talking. What other kinds of secret talking are there?

*** * *

I was sitting on the golden chair in the living room when I heard the knock at the door. It was maybe a week after I stopped talking. Deanna answered the door.

"Hi, Deanna." Margo's voice. "Is Suzie home?"

Send her away. That's what I wanted. *Don't let her in.*

But Deanna opened the door wide, and in came Margo.

"Hi, Suzie," she said. "What's going on?"

I looked at Deanna. Why'd she let Margo in? She knew I couldn't do anything with her. Not even talk.

"Suzie's got a sore throat today," Deanna said after a long five seconds.

"Oh." Margo retreated like I had the plague. Well, Deanna did say I had a sore throat. Maybe she was afraid of catching it. "When you're feeling better, call me, okay?"

I pretended to myself that my neck was too stiff to move, but nodding was talking, and that was the real reason I didn't nod.

Margo backed out the door, but not before I saw tears starting in her eyes. Deanna went with her and closed the door behind them. Good. I knew they were talking about me on the porch, but I didn't care. Now I would be left alone. My cloud gently swirled around me, and I lifted away.

From my height, I saw me in the box with Deanna standing in front of it. She was talking. Gradually the pinkness thinned, so I could make out what she was saying.

"I thought you'd talk if it was one of your friends. I thought you'd try."

Try what? There's nothing to try.

My cloud thickened again, and Deanna's voice was lost in the sounds of the universe. I was happy.

Nothing to try.

❋❋❋

I walk down to the pond with Joshua under trees of red-tinged green. My feet drag, but I walk. Joshua talks most of the time, saying whatever he happens to think. Right now, he's talking about soccer.

"I'm the goalie on my team," he says. "You should see me stop those shots. Nobody can get one past me."

I used to play soccer, too. It seems like a long time ago, before the box closed so tight. Whistles and running, running, running across the field. How did I ever do that? Now my legs are heavy. Walking is hard. Forget running.

It's tough being here with Joshua. I look back at the green bench where I so often sit. I don't like being so far from it. Something like a magnet makes me want to be there. Sitting, quiet and alone. That's what I'm supposed to be doing. That's what I'm best at.

Stella's sitting there now. Of course, her knees are down, and her feet rest on the grass. She would look funny with her knees under her chin in that blue skirt and her bright orangey lipstick. But how come she doesn't have to sit that way? How come I do? Why does that have to be my job?

Stella smiles at me. She makes a sign that I should stay where I am. I know she thinks that if I sit less, I'll break the habit and forget about it. It's not just a habit, though. It's what I do, like drawing or singing or gardening is what other people do that they don't know how not to do. And it's such a fight to stand or walk or do anything else.

"I'm feeling a lot better," says Joshua. "I bet I'll be home as much as I want real soon."

I don't think they'll let *me* go home until I stop sitting, until I start talking. But don't they know they're the same thing?

Karen's right. I'll never go home. I can't do what they want. *Can't.* I have to be the way I am. And what is so wrong with that, with sitting quietly? They don't tell me that. They just don't want me to do it. Why does it bother them?

"I like you," Joshua says. "I'll miss you. You're my friend."

How do you know this?

What he says suddenly means something. My friend is going to go home and not come back. I'll miss him so much!

Oh, these tears!

Another group session. We have one every day. Then lunch. Then time outside or in the solarium. Then dinner. Then bed. Then the next day and another group session. Over and over. What for?

Joshua's talking.

"My dad died." He says it like it's a confession. "He was climbing a mountain with my uncle and—" His voice chokes. Nobody talks while they wait for him to go on. "Dad has asthma. I mean, had it. He forgot his inhaler, and Uncle Blake couldn't get him down the mountain fast enough." He stops and twists his hands together like he's washing them.

"Go on," says Stella.

Go on?! Didn't he say enough? Can't you see it hurts him to tell this?

"Go on," she says.

"So he died. They sat down on some rocks in the middle of nowhere. Uncle Blake said Dad put his head on his shoulder." Joshua stops to take a deep breath. "Uncle Blake put his arm around him, and . . . and . . . and—" Joshua breaks off. We're all silent, and I don't think he's going to finish. How can he? Then he does. "They sat that way together until it was all . . . over."

Joshua puts his head down. Nobody else moves.

I see tears falling into his lap, but he doesn't wipe them away or cover his face. Then he looks up, his face all shiny.

"I was always reminding Dad about his inhaler. I even reminded him before he went with Uncle Blake that time." Joshua's voice is small. "But he left it in the car. I wasn't there to remind him again."

"You couldn't go everywhere with your dad," says Stella. "You weren't responsible for what he did."

"Yeah," says Tina, a real skinny girl. Skinnier even than me. "He was a grown-up. Grown-ups are supposed to remind themselves about stuff they have to do."

"He probably thought he wouldn't need his inhaler." Moses, a little black kid, speaks through a gap in his teeth. His short legs swing over the carpet. "When you feel good, you don't think you're going to be sick in five minutes."

Joshua doesn't answer. Then he looks straight at me.

"Well, all that's what my mother keeps telling me," he says. "About my dad dying, I mean. I don't believe her. She's wrong. She has to be." His voice is defiant. "Dad's coming back!"

"Pretending." Karen mumbles it under her breath. I hope Joshua doesn't hear. I don't want him to hear it, but he does.

"I am NOT pretending!" His fists are clenched, and Karen is laughing.

No, it's my fists that are clenched.

STOP! STOP TALKING!

*** *** ***

Stella's office.

I don't want to be here. I don't want to be anywhere except home. It seems so long since I smelled coffee brewing while I dressed in the morning. So long since I could watch red brake lights shine down at the stop sign. So long since I heard my mother sing, my father snore, Deanna giggle.

No one giggles like Deanna. And no one here giggles at all. I want to hear some giggling.

"You look sad, Suzie," says Stella.

I push away from the homesick feeling and stare at two inches of carpet, look at the evenly cut yarn heads. The yarn heads make a pattern if you look at them long enough. Kind of a backwards *S* that loses shape at the bottom. My eyes try to make the *S* finish its curve, but it disorganizes and falls into nothing every time. I trail back up to the top and follow the line again. It won't work. I stare at it and force the line where it belongs, but when I blink, it's gone. Where's the *S*?

Sad. So sad. The feeling won't go away.

"Look up at me, Suzie."

No.

But I do what she says.

"Do you want to feel better?" Her eyes are so serious, my lower lip begins to shake.

I really do want to feel better. Who wouldn't? I nod my head. Once.

She nods back at me a bunch of times, fast. "Good. Good. Well, you have to try. Are you going to try?"

I nod again. Twice this time. This is talking.

Stella claps her hands, like Marie that first morning when I choked on the orange juice.

A touchdown.

I'm walking with Stella on the sidewalk outside of St. Dorothy's. Leaves rain gently over us, coating the sidewalk in reds, yellows, and oranges. My sandals swish through the growing piles with every shuffling step.

"Lift your feet, Suzie, when you walk."

I don't think I can do that. I look up at Stella.

"You can do it." Her voice is encouraging, cheerful.

I lift my feet high. That's what it feels like, but sometimes I still scrape.

"You're doing fine," says Stella. "You got out of the habit, that's all."

It's the first time I've been away from St. Dorothy's since Uncle Elliot drove me there with Mom and Dad. I don't like being away. It makes me tired to be this far from my bench. I feel like some monster is living in my head, drinking my energy. My neck and back ache from the effort of staying upright. I want to sit down.

Everyone who looks at me can tell something is wrong with me. I'm sure of that. I don't let myself look at anyone. That way, no one can see the monster's mark in my dull black eyes, and I can't see their pity and curiosity.

"I always liked this street." Stella talks to me like she thinks I'm a normal person. I know she knows better. "The buildings are old with lots of decorations on them."

We stop in front of a store with lions' faces carved into the doorway. A satiny pink dress, a frilly pink parasol, and a pair of pink lacy high-button shoes are part of the window display. I imagine myself, my hair swept high and magnificent, wearing the shoes and dress, holding the parasol up to protect my face from the sun. Pretty. I shake my head after a moment. I could never do that. That would *really* be talking.

"Let's go in," says Stella. "This is a thrift shop. They get some interesting things here sometimes."

Inside, it's dark and musty with weak lighting, but I see them right away. Peacock feathers. Bold and exciting. Three of them.

Peacock feathers is talking.

Do the peacocks know this?

I walk past the feathers. Their brilliant colors cling to me, talking, talking, talking.

A mirror above a display of old hats shows my drab, limp hair covering my ears. There is no part.

Hair is talking. I don't like what my hair says.

I watch Stella admiring a green outfit like the one in the window. Her hair is wavy and red, with a sparkly green barrette holding it away from her sparkly eyes.

Stella's hair talks. So do her eyes. Like she's not afraid, like she doesn't know the danger. I think about having hair and eyes like Stella's. Then I feel the yelling and the hitting. I shiver, pushing away the sensation. It's too scary. How come it's not scary for Stella?

I want to sit in a chair. Quiet, quiet, quiet. But there is no chair.

I pick up the peacock feathers and stroke the edges

against my face. So soft. So soft and so blue.

"Do you want them?" asks Stella. "They're pretty, aren't they?"

I put the feathers back. I shouldn't have picked them up. I should have known better. I hunch my shoulders and wait.

"It's okay to want them," Stella says. She tilts her head down to look at me. "I'd never be mad if you wanted them. Do you? They're almost free."

I nod and slowly put my shoulders down while she smiles and smiles at me.

Suddenly, I know I'm safe with her. A five-hundred-pound weight falls off my shoulders, and tears fill my eyes with relief. *Safe.* I'd forgotten how it felt. Did I ever know?

Stella pays the lady for the feathers, and we leave the shop.

Outside, I look through the peacock feathers at the pink display.

"You'd look pretty in that outfit," says Stella. "You in the pink and me in the green. Wouldn't that be fun?"

If I only dared.

*** *** ***

My mother's pretty. That's where Deanna gets her looks. But Mom's hair is short and curly. Not real short, but real curly. Wild, you might say.

And her eyes are blue like Deanna's, only not as dark. Mom's eyes have little glints of green in them, too, so sometimes they look like the Atlantic Ocean. She loves to wear blue-green.

I borrowed one of her skirts one day. I didn't have one I liked, and I needed one for the school trip to see *Phantom of the Opera*. Blues and greens swirled through a paisley pattern, and I felt beautiful. But when I came downstairs and Mom saw which skirt I borrowed, I could see her mouth tighten.

"You know what?" I thought fast. "This skirt's too tight around the middle. I think I'll wear my orange jumper after all."

Mom smiled, and I went back upstairs. I wondered what about wearing that skirt made Mom angry, but mostly I felt relieved. She wouldn't hit me in my old orange thing.

Back in my room at St. Dorothy's, I look at myself in the mirror. I don't like my hair, hanging any old way. I pick up my comb.

But if I fix my hair, that's talking.

I put the comb down. I look in the mirror again. If I don't fix it, that's talking, too. I don't like what it says. But people will notice if I make it better. Someone will say something. Someone will hurt me.

No! Don't think that!

Who? Who will hurt me if I comb my hair?

No one, I tell myself quickly. No one here. I push the images, red and black, away.

But someone will notice. They notice things here.

So what? I try out that question. So what? Other people say that. Can I?

How important is my hair to anyone, anyway? And maybe no one will notice.

I pick up the comb. No one's looking right now. Not in my room. If I do it by myself, is it talking?

I start combing. It takes a long time to comb out all the knots. When I'm finished, my scalp tingles. My hair feels lighter. It feels good. I dip my head so I can comb a straight part, right down the middle. Then I check the mirror again. My hair shines in the light. I like the way it looks.

But hair is talking if I leave my room. My stomach hurts when I open my door, so I close it again. I sit on my bed.

What should I do? Then I remember the peacock feathers on the bureau. I grab them and put them in front of my face, looking through them. They talk louder than my hair. They're what people will notice.

But Jody says, "I like your hair" when we pass in the hall. I keep on, my feet going *sh-sh, sh-sh,* but I wait for something else from Jody.

I think of Jody rocking and rocking me. She won't yank my hair or laugh. Right? Can you rock someone and hurt them, too?

"Nice hair," says Edgar in the art room. What does he mean by that? My box closes in. I sit with my knees under my chin.

He draws me a picture of a girl with light shiny hair parted in the middle. He puts a big smile on her face. He writes BEAUTIFUL BLACK-EYED SUZIE at the bottom. Then he holds the picture out to me. I take it and stare at it. It makes me feel good to look at it. I decide to keep that picture forever.

*** * ***

One time at Margo's house, her dad was playing an instrumental on the stereo. I wasn't paying attention to much except being stretched out on the carpet with my hand of gin rummy.

"Your turn," I said.

"So what?" sang Margo.

"Huh?"

She conducted the music for a couple of beats. I put my hand down and listened. The back-and-forth playing of the instruments sounded like two people talking:

"If you don't wash the dishes, you'll get in trouble."

"So what?" Sassy.

"If you don't study, you'll flunk the . . ."

"So what?"

"It's raining, and the leaves are falling . . ."

"So what?"

Margo sang the "so what" part each time. Pretty soon I was singing it, too. Then we started filling in the other part.

"If you don't brush your teeth, you'll get . . ."

"So what?"

"Then your teeth will fall out and . . ."

"So what?"

"Then you'll look like a witch and you'll . . ."

"So what?"

But then we couldn't even get out the "so what" part, so we were laughing so hard. And each time the music played it, we laughed harder. We were rolling around on the floor, practically busting our guts, when Margo's dad came into the room and stared at us.

"What's the joke?" he asked.

"So what?" Margo burst out, and we were off again.

He looked puzzled for a second. "Oh," he said. "It's the music."

"Huh?" I rolled to a sitting position. How did he know what we were doing?

"It's called 'So What?' That's the name of it," Margo's dad explained.

Then the music played "so what," and Margo and I were gone again.

We never finished that game of gin.

❋❋❋

I'm carrying the feathers and Edgar's picture back to my room. Karen's angry voice shouts from a room down the hall.

"Well, I won't!" she yells.

Slam! And she appears.

I walk the other way as fast as I can because I don't want to be near Karen. But I can't get my legs to speed up. They won't do it. I might as well be trying to outrun a race car.

I hold the picture and the feathers close to my body and aim for the next doorway. I'm almost there when Karen catches me.

"Scared?" She pushes me, cracking my head against the wall. She yanks the paper from me and it tears. I just have a few strips in my hands now, with the feathers, while she stares at what Edgar drew.

"Beautiful black-eyed Suzie," she says. "More like ugly black-eyed Suzie, or stupid dumb-eyed Suzie. Ha-ha-haah!"

Then, right before my nose—*No!*—she tears the picture in half. Then in half again. My picture. I wanted that.

"What are you going to do about that, beautiful Suzie? Huh, Suzie, what?" Her breath is so close I can smell it.

She tears the paper until all she has are little pieces. She throws them into the air, and they whirl down like pinwheels to the floor.

"So there, Suzie!" She kicks the scraps so they scatter.

I don't want to cry, but she's got me so scared.

"I'll give you something to cry about," she snarls.

I see the fist coming, but not in time. She punches the right side of my jaw, but that's as far as she gets before Marie grabs her. Karen's skirt flips up over her underpants while she kicks and screams against Marie's iron grip. Marie just keeps walking, walking.

My face hurts all over. I hold it in my hands.

Bill squats to get me to look at him while he says, "Don't be scared, Suzie. It's all right. It's all right."

I don't believe him.

＊＊＊

On the bench outside, the peacock feathers move in the breeze. I follow the smoothness of them, each one so perfectly made, with my fingers. Then I sit back, watching the clouds curling and uncurling, unpredictable and perfect. How can the clouds be unpredictable and perfect if the feathers are always perfectly the same?

"It's going to rain." Joshua's voice. "Feel that wind?"

The bench shifts when he sits next to me, but I watch the clouds and touch the feathers.

It's going to rain? Perfect and unpredictable, curling and uncurling until the curls straighten to fall down as wet and clear as an idea thought all the way through.

"Pretty peacock feathers," says Joshua. "Where did you get them?"

Joshua knows I don't talk. But I know he asks questions anyway.

That's okay.

We're not perfect.

***

I'm holding the peacock feathers in the solarium when Deanna visits again.

"Peacock feathers! Let me see."

I don't give them to her, but Deanna takes them out of my hands. Gramps's ring is on her finger. I remember it glinting in the light when he read me stories a long time ago. I wish it was mine, but Mom gave it to Deanna when he died.

"What do you need peacock feathers for in a place like this?"

She holds the feathers up to my face and crosses her eyes at me through them. I can tell she thinks the feathers don't exactly go with me the way icing goes with cake. They go with her. If it's pretty, it's hers.

I know this. That's the way things have always been, and should be. Peacock feathers do go better with flashing blue eyes and black hair. With someone who is alive every minute. Someone everyone loves.

Deanna puts the feathers on the table.

"So, how long are you going to do this? Give everyone the silent treatment. Mom says you're punishing her."

Why does Mom say this? Does Deanna believe it, too? I'm trying my best, but everything is so hard. Can't they see that? I still drag my feet when I walk unless I really think about it.

And I can't talk.

Why do people think I won't?

How can I be punishing anyone? I'm the brown dot in the box.

"Listen, Suzie, I know it's hard living in our house." Deanna wets her lips like she's nervous. "But you gotta come back. With me being the only kid, I don't like it. You don't know what Mom's been like with only me there. I can't bring my friends home anymore, the way she screams all the time. She's just mad, no matter what. If you were there, she'd calm down. We could help each other."

She looks searchingly at me when I don't answer. What does she want?

"Oh, Suzie. Have I lost you? Now I'm going to lose my friends, too."

Friends. Joshua's my friend. I don't want to lose him. I don't want Deanna to lose her friends. But why does she think I'm lost? I'm right here. Not lost. Am I lost? What's lost? Lost is dark, black, with no light. Maybe I am lost. Something makes my breath quicken and my eyes water.

"I'm sorry, Suzie. I shouldn't have said that. You aren't really lost. You'll be back."

Deanna wipes my eyes with a tissue from her purse.

"It's just that everything's mixed up and different. It's making me crazy."

Deanna's not crazy. I'm the crazy one.

"Please, Suzie, why won't you talk?"

I look at Deanna. My looking at her without talking makes her suddenly real upset, like something hits her. Her face gets red, and she blinks her eyes real fast.

Deanna tries to pick up her purse, but she doesn't see it right because she's blinking her eyes. She knocks it off the table. Then she knocks over a chair, trying to pick it up.

I know she's clumsy because she's all upset and because she's afraid she'll cry in front of everyone. Not that many people here would care. I would care, though. I don't like Deanna to cry. She throws the strap of the purse over her left shoulder and stands up, knocking the chair over again. Somehow, her purse opens, and everything falls out all over the table.

She is crying now, but she's trying to smile, to pretend she's not crying. Tears don't go with that perky blue and green sports outfit. She picks up all her junk and stuffs it back into her purse. She picks up everything nearby, too. I don't think she even knows she's holding three crayons and my feathers. Fine. Let her have them.

"Well, Suzie," she says. Her voice is high and scratchy. "I'll see you later."

She clamps her mouth shut to keep the crying quiet, but she can't help one loud sob. I feel bad that she's so unhappy. I wish there was something I could do.

Stella stops her at the door.

"I'm sorry." Her words are quiet. "But you've got Suzie's peacock feathers."

Deanna looks down, surprised to see them. She brings them back to me and puts them on the table. She puts the three crayons next to them like she never saw them before.

"Suzie." She looks down at me. "I wish you'd come home. I miss you."

I see Stella standing at the door, like a guard. She smiles at me and nods. I pick up one feather and offer it to Deanna. She looks from the feather to me.

"Oh, Suzie!" She runs for the door without taking the feather. Then she comes back slowly. "Are you giving me this feather?"

I still hold it out to her.

I know giving is talking, but Stella is there. It's safe with Stella. I can give. And Deanna is suffering so much.

Deanna takes the feather gently.

"Oh, Suzie!" But this time she whispers, brushing my cheek with the feather. Then she kisses where the feather touched. "I'll save this forever!"

This time she does leave, but she's not running. She waves to me from the door, smiling. She waves the feather.

Walking is easier. I don't have to think so much about it. I feel my feet rise and fall, one-and-two-and-one-and-two, on the square-patterned linoleum floor.

The art room has some new kids in it today, but I don't see Joshua. I wonder where he is. Karen's here, but she's quiet, keeping her back to the rest of us. Good. Maybe they've got her on some anti-mean medicine now, instead of the happy pills.

I sit next to Moses. He's moving his elbows in rhythm to a song he's humming. He has a cheerful, squeaky hum.

"Feel like drawing today?" Edgar asks. "How about a ghost or a witch to help us decorate for Halloween?"

He always asks, but I don't draw.

Edgar's voice is soft. Most of the time, if he's not laughing, he looks like he's about to. I wish he'd sing Joshua's funny song with that soft voice.

"That's a cool giraffe," he says to Moses.

I don't know how he knows it's a giraffe. It looks like a bunch of scribbles to me. But Moses stops humming to grin up at Edgar, and I like that. Not many of the children here grin.

I want to make Moses grin at me.

While Edgar leans over Karen's table, I draw a peacock feather. It's my first picture. I sweat while I draw, checking every few seconds on Edgar's turned back. My stomach tightens, but I still draw. I finish and lay down the crayons, lined up one by one. I'm very tired, and my hand aches.

I'm also surprised. Who would think drawing a picture could make you so tired?

I look at the picture. It's a peacock feather. That's all. But I like it. I give it to Moses. I get that grin, showing the gap in Moses' front teeth. I love that grin.

I take that grin and put it on my face. I show it to Edgar when he comes back. Edgar looks shocked. So does Karen. I almost laugh, but not quite.

Then, "Way to go, girl, way to go!" And Edgar has that laughing face again.

Joshua's outside, sitting on a bench by himself. He's leaning against the wood slats, his legs stretched out. Staring, staring. The soccer ball sits by itself in the middle of the courtyard, the sun shining off it, but he's not staring at that.

I sit next to Joshua. He looks over at me.

"Hi, Suzie," he says. "My father is dead. He's never coming back. He isn't."

He doesn't cry. He doesn't move, either, like he has a great pain starting in his stomach and reaching like a star through his whole body.

I want him to feel better.

Where are my words? I need my words.

I take Joshua's hand in mine and look into his bloodshot gray eyes.

"Sorry." I found a word. I don't know where it came from. It was just there. One word. Mostly, it doesn't come out, just the "ry" part. "Sorry."

Joshua straightens up, staring at me. He's not sure he heard me. Then he is. What's he going to do? I'm scared.

I pull my hand away and cover my burning face. My knees are up to my chin, my feet on the bench. I wait for the scalding scorn and for the pain that always comes.

Please. Please don't.

"What's the matter, Joshua?" It's Stella's voice, but I don't look, can't look.

The box closes in, pushing, pushing against me everywhere so I'm small, but not small enough. I'm still, sitting in the smallest space I can, waiting. I wish I could be stiller, smaller, invisible, not here.

Why did I speak?

"Joshua?"

"She said something," he says. "I told her my dad was dead. She said, 'Sorry.' Twice!"

Oh, no, oh, no.

"Why is she so afraid?" he asks. "I'm not going to hit her."

"Some people were pretty mean to her," says Stella. "Isn't that right, Suzie?"

I stay tight, not moving. Maybe they'll go away. Maybe I'll die. I want to die. Why did I talk? Why was I born? Please, let me die.

"Don't be afraid," says Joshua. "I'm happy you said that. Stella's happy, too, aren't you?"

"Of course."

Do they mean that? Or are they just waiting to catch me at something worse to make their words more stinging, to make the hits harder? I look between my fingers.

Stella's face is worried, not mad, and I remind myself that I'm safe with her. I don't always hold that thought very well. She won't hurt me. Neither will Joshua. I'm safe with him, too.

I close my eyes again quick, but I know they saw me looking. I'm safe, I tell myself with my eyes shut tight, but I'm scared anyway.

Someone's rubbing my arm. It's Stella.

"Don't be afraid," she says. "We won't hurt you."

I bring my hands down. Then my legs.

My stomach hurts.

"We won't ever hurt you," says Joshua.

Still, my stomach hurts.

✳✳✳

Deanna's here again. She has a new boyfriend, Kenny.

"He's waiting for me in the parking lot," Deanna says. "See him?" She points to someone washing the windshield of a small yellow car. "He's so proud of that car. Took him two years to save up for it, working all the time."

We stay at the solarium window, watching the day.

"I put my peacock feather on my bureau," she says. "It's so pretty. Oh! I almost forgot. I brought you a gift."

She pulls something out of her purse and hands it to me. It's a small hand mirror.

"Turn it over," she says.

The back is decorated with purple irises in enamel. I trace the lines of the flowers.

"I saw it in one of those specialty shops at the mall," says Deanna. "It has your name all over it."

I love it. I look up at Deanna, wishing I could tell her.

"You really like it, don't you?"

Before I can think at all, a small hand shoots in front of my eyes and grabs the mirror. It's gone! Karen has it, and she's running for the exit, laughing. Deanna and Bill chase her to the hallway. Deanna comes back alone, angry. I'm angry, too.

"I don't like you being in this place," Deanna says. "You shouldn't be living this way. People stealing from you like that."

Tell me about it.

"Oh, look!" Deanna points out the window.

Karen's outside, running. Boy, is she fast! Bill's never going to catch her, even with his long legs. Why does he even bother trying? She can't go anywhere, not with that fence everywhere. He should just wait until she gets tired.

Oh. That's why. She's climbing a tree, climbing and climbing. She's way up there, peeking around the trunk to grin at Deanna and me at the window. She flashes the mirror at us. Then she throws it. It arcs through the air until it smashes against the fence. Even from here, I can see the pieces fly apart. Why'd she have to do that?

Deanna pulls me to a table where we can't see Karen, and we sit down. I'm angry.

"Forget her," says Deanna. "Little creep. I'll get you another mirror."

I want that *one.*

Karen. I hope she stays up in that tree the rest of her life.

I feel so tired. I'm having trouble eating again. At lunch, the only thing I could eat before my throat closed up was three tomato slices.

Everybody's asking me questions, trying to get me to talk. Not like usual, but all the time. They won't leave me alone. They're all like Karen—pushing and pushing at me. I want to go home where no one will bother me.

Just because I talked once doesn't mean I can talk more. I don't own the words.

Stella says I have to try. But try what? Either I own the words or I don't. Can you make a river run without water?

"You can do it," Stella says.

Without water?

I open my mouth, bite my lower lip, then my upper lip. How do you do it?

I look at Stella. She is disappointed, I can tell. She thought one word meant a waterfall.

"Your eyes are so sad," she says. "If I knew what made them sad, I could help more. You don't have to live with such sadness."

I lower my eyes to hide the sadness Stella sees. I stare at the toy train on the table in her office. I wish I could ride it out of St. Dorothy's. Ride it home to my golden chair.

"Trust me," Stella says.

Trust. That makes me think of a loaf of good crusty bread, warm and rich when you open it up. I take that word with me when I leave Stella's office, making sure to pick up my feet from the floor with each step. I think about that word. It's not new, but it feels new.

Trust.

***

I'm lying down on my bench. I'm too tired to sit up. The word *trust* sits on top of me like a gigantic bear, making all my bones hurt. The sun is shining, and there is a breeze rustling the weeping willow leaves overhead. I want the sun to warm me, to take away the aches.

Joshua comes outside with his soccer ball. I realize I've never seen him without it. Even drawing pictures with Edgar, he has it.

He sits cross-legged on the grass in front of my bench because I'm taking up the whole thing.

"What's the matter?" he asks. "You look like you fell out of that tree."

He glances up.

"Nah. The branches are too high. You'd look worse."

He's trying to make a joke, but it's too much work to smile.

He knows I wouldn't be climbing trees, anyway. My box wouldn't let me do that. Not that he sees the box, but he knows what it does.

How come he can tell what I feel like? I'm just lying here.

"That meant a lot to me yesterday," he says. "When you said, 'Sorry'."

I look at him through my hair.

"It made me feel good that you did that. It must be about the hardest thing you ever did."

The sunlight makes my hair glow, and I see Joshua through a soft cloud.

"I'll always remember that you did such a hard thing for me."

The cloud caresses Joshua's face. I reach out my hand and touch the cloud.

I sit up fast. What did I do?

Joshua grins at me. Did I touch his face? I've never touched a boy's face before.

He reaches out and touches my face, too, then brushes hair out of my eyes. At first I'm scared, but his hand is gentle. Only gentle.

I feel a peace settle down on me. I am safe with Joshua.

Friend. I don't have to say it. But I have the word.

"Friend," he says. Like he knows.

*** *** ***

Outside, I watch Joshua and Moses pass the soccer ball
back and forth. The air is cold, and my hands hurt even
though they're in pockets. I'm standing near the bench,
practicing not sitting on it. What is it that makes me want
to fold up there?

The hospital door opens. Oh, no, not Karen. Ugh. There's
that awful laugh. They must be trying her on another new
medicine. Or maybe she spits out the ones they give her
when no one's looking. Why does she want to be so mean?

She points at me. Uh-oh. Grown-ups are here, but they
won't be able to stop her. I walk behind the bench to put it
between Karen and me. I wish I could run.

She charges down the steps, still laughing. She never
slows down until she gets to Moses. She pushes him down
and grabs the soccer ball.

"Hey!" from Joshua.

She runs to my bench and leaps onto it. She raises the
ball and aims it at my face.

I cross my hands over my face and squinch my eyes shut.
Please don't hurt me! My hands, my face! Don't!

"What's the matter?" Karen asks. "Don't you trust me?"

I open my eyes in time to see Karen throw the ball away
toward the fence.

She jumps down and runs to elude Bill, but Bill catches
her and half carries her back inside. She cackles all the way.

She's crazy.

Hmm. Look who's—umm—not talking.

I haven't seen Mom for a long time. Why doesn't she visit? I miss her and Deanna all the time.

I wish I could be home with them, in the living room with the golden, curvy wallpaper and the curtains that match. It's a pretty room. I can sit in it. Nobody will ask me to talk. Nobody will ask me to do anything. Mostly. And no Karens will be there to knock me around or wreck my stuff.

It's my home. I belong there.

Stella says I'm making progress. I'm walking better and eating more. I'm sleeping, mostly on my own. I'm not crying very much, so I guess I'm feeling better. Sometimes I can tell.

But this is what worries me. I'm moving farther and farther away from who I am and what I should be doing. That's what the people here want me to do, to change, to move away from what I was. But I so long for the gold-upholstered chair in the living room. It fits me just right. When I go home, I'll go straight to that chair. I don't know what else I could do. It will be such a relief to do what I'm supposed to do and not fight to be different.

Maybe Stella knows this. Maybe that's why I'm still here.

❋ ❋ ❋

Uncle Elliot is here. He brought me some candy bars and a tee shirt. This one has an eagle flying across it. He's wearing an eagle shirt himself, but it's for the football team. Mine's not.

"You're the eagle," he says. "I'm the eagle's fan."

I smile. I like that.

"You're looking much better." He glances out over St. Dorothy's grounds from my bench under the weeping willow. Joshua's teaching Moses how to dribble the soccer ball, and there's a new girl in a wheelchair being pushed towards the pond. "I'm very pleased," Uncle Elliot says.

I think I am feeling better. I'm not always sure, and I'm not always sure what it is I need to feel better than. But my shoulders feel lighter. How can that make sense?

"I bought you and Deanna new bikes," he says.

Oh! I bring my feet up quick.

"Now, don't do that," he says. "If you don't like yours, I can take it back."

Take it back! Take it back! I don't want another bike. Mom will . . .

"But Aunt Olga and I thought we'd take you girls on some bike hikes when you get your strength back." He spreads a pamphlet out on his lap. Pictures of green and gold trees against blue skies. "Isn't this beautiful? There's an old inn at the end of this trail. They serve hot cider in the fall."

I stare at the pictures. I can almost taste that cider. Hot cider's the best.

Then I think of the bike. But it will be at Uncle Elliot's, right? Mom might not know.

I begin to relax.

"We're going to do lots of good things together when you're better," says Uncle Elliot. "I promise. You think about things you want to do, too, and we'll do 'em."

Things I want to do? What could that be?

But the images race across my brain. Running, laughing, So What-ing.

"I can't get over the change in you," says Uncle Elliot.

I wonder what Mom was crocheting with that green and white yarn the last time I saw her. Is she still angry? Every day I think she'll come, but she never does. Maybe she's sick. But somebody would tell me that, right?

She sang to me when I was little. Or at least she sang. I loved to listen, snuggled against my pillow at night. The warm sounds washed over me, soothing as a salve. So beautiful. When she sang, I forgot how angry she could be other times. When she sang, she was perfect.

I sang, too, to be like her.

"Oh, Suzie, stop. It's terrible," she would say. "It hurts my ears."

I would look up at her, my legs dangling from the piano bench. She'd have her hands over her ears. Her face would look like she had something sharp stuck into her.

Then she would laugh, but her laugh was harsh and brittle, not like her singing. Frost would settle on my heart.

I stopped singing when she was home. Then I stopped singing altogether. Because even if she wasn't home, I could hear her laugh. I couldn't take that laugh. I felt so cold underneath it.

Tonight, I hear Moses singing in his room. He slides around the pitches, but I don't care. He sounds happy.

***

Dad's here. What do I do with him? He's sitting with me outside on a bench, but he's not saying anything, either. Did he miss me?

Then finally he says, "They tell me you said a couple of words. That's good. Soon you'll be a regular chatterbox like before."

I was never a chatterbox. Why do you say that?

And why hasn't he come to see me in so long? He and Mom hardly come here at all.

He leans against the back of the bench and crosses his legs.

"It's still so warm this fall," he says. "We haven't had a hard frost yet, and here it is November."

November. I'm missing a lot of school. How will I catch up?

Dad clears his throat. "Suzie," he says. His head is down so he's almost looking at me through his eyebrows.

What?

I feel like something weird is about to happen.

"The Child Welfare people are giving us a hard time," he says. "I guess you know that."

How would I?

He looks straight at me. "You're not an abused child, you know. If people are telling you that, don't listen. Somehow, people got the wrong idea. It's got Mom all upset."

But . . .

"I told them," he goes on, "I've never seen your mother

lay a hand on you or Deanna. She would never hurt anyone, especially one of her daughters. That's what I said."

What is he talking about? She hits him, too. What about that day . . .

"Well, I know," he adds, "that's not exactly true. But we have to say it because . . . well, it's protecting our family. I mean, Mom's not abusive or anything. And if we say she ever hits anyone, then that makes trouble. Do you understand?"

I do understand. More than he thinks. But I don't nod or anything. I don't like what I understand. He's afraid to stand up to Mom. Someone should stand in her way. If he doesn't, who?

"So watch what you say when you start talking again, okay? We don't want to get Mom all upset. Right? You know how she gets."

The box squeezes in on me. I sit close and tight. What else can I do?

Karen runs across the courtyard and stops dead in front of us.

"Why is Suzie holding her legs so hard?" She kicks Dad on the shin. "What did you do to her?"

He smiles at her like she hadn't kicked him and stands up.

"She always sits like that," he says.

"No she doesn't." Karen sticks her chin way out. "Hardly ever any more."

Why does *she* care?

Dad acts like he doesn't hear her. He takes his suit jacket from the bench and slings it over his shoulder.

Something bad is happening here.

"Well, Suzie, gotta go." He kisses me on the cheek and leaves.

Karen picks up something from the ground and hurls it after him—a pebble, maybe. It hits Dad square on the back, leaving a mark against his light-blue shirt, but he doesn't turn around. Just keeps going right out the gate.

Karen's looking at me. "Stop doing that!" she hollers.

What? I'm not doing anything.

She grabs one of my ankles and yanks my leg away from my body. Then the other, and she's pushing on my knees to keep my feet on the ground. I've lost my balance, and I'm falling to the side. She doesn't let go. How can this scrawny kid be so strong?

Huge hands appear suddenly, covering hers. Karen lets go, and Bill backs her away from me.

"Oh, Karen," he sighs. "Thelma!" he calls to the other aide.

Karen screams words so high and scratchy I can't understand them while he carries her back to the building. She's hitting and kicking him, but that doesn't slow Bill down at all. He hardly seems to notice. Doesn't even look mad.

By the time the other aide reaches me, I'm back the way I was, tightly folded up inside the box.

"Are you all right?" asks Thelma.

Pieces of pink and gold nestle against me this time, all warm and soft. Ahh . . .

***

I was raking leaves out back. Dad wanted them raked into a pile, but I missed the ones in the garden.

"How could you miss them?" he asked. "Is it that you're lazy?"

I didn't answer, just swallowed hard. I'm not lazy.

"Now, don't look hurt."

So I pretended to smile and went to the garden. I made sure I raked with my back to Dad so he couldn't see my hurt face.

But I *was* hurt. Shouldn't I get to look that way?

***

Uncle Elliot came over to see Dad on the coldest day last February. Dad wasn't home yet, and Mom was out shopping. I was making chocolate chip cookies and drinking hot chocolate while Deanna did her homework at the kitchen table. I made a mug for Uncle Elliot, too.

"I met a bear outside," said Uncle Elliot.

"Sure," I said. I pulled the second batch out of the oven. When I turned around again, Uncle Elliot was chewing on a cookie from the first batch.

"He said it was so cold, his paws were sticking to the sidewalk. He's heading south, over the mountains." Then Uncle Elliot started singing. "The bear went over the mountain, the bear went over the mountain, the bear went over the mountain . . ." Uncle Elliot conducted his song with his cookie. Deanna and I laughed when Uncle Elliot changed the words. "To see if he could get warm."

"Nice rhyme," commented Deanna.

"Oh, well." Uncle Elliot took a sip of his chocolate before he started singing again. I sang with him. "The bear went over the mountain, the bear went over the mountain, the bear went over the mountain . . ."

He paused while I finished.

"To see how many chocolate chip cookies he could steal." I squeezed the words together so they'd fit the melody.

Mom came in on my last words. I hadn't heard the front door open.

"Suzie, cut out that racket. It's terrible."

"Hello, Corynne," said Uncle Elliot. "You don't like our music?"

Mom jumped at Uncle Elliot's voice. She hadn't noticed him sitting at the counter by the door.

"What are you doing here?" Her eyes were narrow.

I looked at Deanna. Her eyes met mine for one second before she glued them to her book. I went back to dropping dough on the cookie sheet.

"I have something to give Alex. Your darling daughters are keeping me entertained with cookies and song while I wait."

"Entertained!" Mom snorted. "More likely tortured, with that voice of Suzie's."

"Corynne!"

Mom sang the opening of the bear song, imitating my voice. I guess I sounded like a crow to her. I tried not to listen.

"Corynne, stop that! You're hurting her feelings."

"I am not! It's only the truth. And don't you tell me how to behave! What do you know about it?"

Then Mom really started yelling. Stuff about Dad and his job and how Uncle Elliot thought he could interfere any way he wanted.

Uncle Elliot didn't move, but his cookie broke from his fingers and fell onto the counter. I stood quietly, staring at the floor with the filled cookie sheet in my hand. I felt a tug on my arm. Silently, Deanna took the sheet from me and put it down. She pulled me out the back door.

We stood on the frozen ground, breathing white from our mouths. I noticed that Deanna was wearing only socks on her feet. It made me even colder to see that.

"I wish we lived in the South," said Deanna. "It's too cold here."

Mom's angry voice carried right out. I was glad we couldn't understand what she said. Finally, we heard the front door open, then slam, before Uncle Elliot's car started and took off.

"I wonder what he wanted to give Dad," I said.

"I think it was a check," said Deanna.

The house was quiet a long time before Deanna opened the back door a crack. We could hear Mom's telephone voice. Safe to go in.

I didn't see Uncle Elliot again until the day he brought me here.

***

Joshua bounces his ball on the bench between us. I wish he wouldn't. I can't sit right with all that bouncing.

"Watch, Suzie."

He leaves the bench to kick the ball into the air. Each time it comes down, he kicks it again. *Bam, bam, bam.* It never touches the ground.

"Pretty good, huh?" he says, out of breath. "That was fifteen times. I've made it up to twenty."

His cheeks are pink, his eyes sparkle. He's not laughing— at least not out loud. But his body is laughing. It makes me want to laugh, too.

He hits the ball into the air with his head. One, two, three, four, five times before it falls.

"That's harder," he says.

He comes back to sit again.

"I'll tell you something," he says. "I don't like head balls so much. They make my head hurt after awhile."

Well, naturally.

I start to laugh. I can't help it. Joshua stares at me like he's afraid there's something wrong. Then he starts to laugh, too. Pretty soon, we're laughing together like a couple of regular people.

***

I think about Moses singing. I want to sing, too, but I have no words. I can think of no songs. Even Joshua's silly song flies away when I try to think of it.

Maybe if I sing without words, I can do it.

But if I sing, I will make ugly sounds. People will be angry.

But if I hum softly, no one will hear.

I climb into my bed and hum into the pillow. At first, there is no sound, only the sound in my head. Then there is a sound, raspy and low, like a rusty gate. The notes come in no particular order. But it doesn't matter. I hum for a long time.

***

The sunbeam breaks across the empty solarium when I come in. I stand at the window, soaking up the spreading gold. The kids I see on the grass below are wearing heavy jackets, but I'm warm where I am.

Mm-mm-mm . . .

My humming sounds different here—echoey and loud. No one's here but me, though. It's all right.

Mmm-mm.

Can't remember any tunes. Just having fun finding notes. Sounds without words. Talking without talking. Funny.

I laugh a little.

"What's funny?"

I spin. There's Karen. She's on the floor, looking at me from behind a big chair. She's probably been there the whole time.

She crawls out and stands up. "What's funny?" I said. Her knees are grimy, her feet are bare, and her chin's almost pointing straight out.

I shake my head, edging for the door. There's something bad wrong with Karen, and I'm not going to be alone with her if I can help it.

"You can hum and laugh, but you can't talk? I don't believe you. You think we're all stupid enough to believe that?"

I don't care what she believes. I have to get out of here.

But she blocks my way. There is only one way out.

Why choose me? Why bother with me at all? I lift my chin and point it at her. *Hah! So there!*

Her curls are even wilder than usual. I wonder if she can get a comb through them. Narrowed eyes almost disappear in that angry face. She was born angry, I bet. It isn't about me at all.

Karen shakes a fist in my face.

"What's funny?" she repeats. "Tell me, or you'll get it."

Then I do get it. I really get it. She's going to hit me unless I tell her something funny? Now *that's* funny. Everything is funny. Her, her questions, me, the whole thing. I would laugh, except for the unfunny part where her fist is.

A streak of white anger flashes through me. How dare she mess with me?

I grab her wrist and drag her across the floor. She resists and fights me all the way, but my anger makes me strong. She won't hit me again.

I thrust her out the door into Marie's path. There are two people in winter clothes with Marie.

"Karen!" cries the man. "Here you are!"

The woman I don't know opens her arms, inviting a hug against soft fur. "How's my girl?"

For a split second after I drop her wrist, Karen is still. Then—*Zoom!*—she flies down the hall, the light shining on those long bare legs. *Slam!* She's out the door to the courtyard.

"No better, huh?" The man's tone is odd, like he's making a joke. "Still the little monkey we all know and love."

"Donald!" The woman looks nervously at Marie and me. Why does she care what I think?

I return to the window in the solarium. The sun is still warm through the window, but Karen must be cold in the crook of that tree with bare feet and no coat. I bet she stays there an hour after those awful people drive away.

***

It's bedtime, and I sit on my bed. I push the walls of my box with my hands. The walls are hard and rough, like raw wood. They move a little. I push again. They don't move.

What would life be like if there was no box? What would I be if I didn't have to sit, if that wasn't my job? If you take away the box and the job, what would be left of me? Would I die? Would I lose shape and trickle away to evaporate like water escaping from a riverbed? I always think so.

But . . . what if I didn't?

I'm holding on to the edge of the mattress real tight. These are scary thoughts. But I don't let go of the mattress or my thoughts.

I slow my thinking down so I can turn over every idea to examine it like a cube of swirled colors. If you . . . take away the box . . . and the chair . . . won't I . . . still . . . be here? They aren't me, right? They're just layers, right? So who am I, *what* am I, underneath?

I picture a small heart lit from inside to a pale gold. It beats. It's alive, waiting to grow.

I am the heart. The box and the chair hold me down, but I am . . . alive . . . underneath.

Alive!

I knocked over three chairs in the solarium before I went outside this morning. I tried to knock over the bench under the weeping willow tree. It's cemented into the ground somehow, and I couldn't budge it. I cut my hand trying.

Now I knock over a chair in Stella's office and sit on the floor. I stand up. I lean against the wall. The wall is in the way. I push on it like it's my box, but it won't move.

"Let's go outside," says Stella. "You need space."

Outside, it is raining. I don't care. Stella walks under an umbrella, but I don't want one. I stretch my arms in every direction. The only limitation is the ground. I stamp on the ground and jump away from it. But I know everyone is tied to the ground. Not to chairs or benches or boxes. Maybe being tied to the ground is okay, but I wish I could fly into outer space.

"You look really mad," says Stella.

Mad. I *am* mad. Why do I have to be a chair sitter? Why can't I play soccer like Joshua and have a pink, happy face?

We come to the bench. I kick the seat. I kick it twice. That hurts my foot, but I don't care. I kick the bench again.

Why do I have to be quiet? Why do I have to sit? Why can't I talk and sing and yell and holler?

Being mad is talking, and I don't care. I want to talk.

Death to all chairs.

We walk over to the pond. The ducks act like they don't care that it's raining. They stick their bottoms up in the water like normal. They quack like normal. They sit on the bank like normal, putting up with the rain on their soft, speckled brown backs.

It's not fair. I feel so awful, and everything is just normal for them.

I don't want them to sit there like that. I want them to fly away. I want to take away their pond.

I want . . . I want . . .

I sit on the wet bank with the ducks and sob. I don't know what I want. I just want things to be better. My slacks are soaked, but I don't care.

"Let's go inside," says Stella. "Dry is better."

I get up and follow her inside. What else can I do?

❋❋❋

I'm inside. In dry clothes, wearing my eagle shirt. But what I'm really wearing is my cloud. I bring it all around me, calling in more and more layers until there is nothing anywhere but misty, foamy pink. I lean against it, letting it carry me high, so high.

Higher and higher I go. Out of St. Dorothy's, above and away, like a silvery pink balloon. High into the universe I go, with nothing to hold me. Away from boxes, away from talking, away from people, away from caring . . .

Anger, fear, unhappiness—they all go away, staying in my box on the ground. Good-bye, brown ugly box. You can't hold me down.

Ahh . . .

So peaceful. I'm never coming back. Never, never. I'm like the light of a setting sun—once gone, forever gone. I will never come back.

I settle in for eternity.

"Suzie? Suzie?" Something warm pats my face.

The sound of running. Another voice. "What happened?"

"I don't know. I found her like this."

I look up from the cold linoleum floor. My cloud is moving away. Hey, come back! Come back!

I cry because people keep talking, and my cloud thins to nothing, and I'm so tired of everything not working.

I want my mother.

***

One time when I was nine, I got kicked in the head playing soccer. I'd just made the perfect slide tackle, but the other kid's foot clipped me as he flew over. I don't actually remember how I got hit, but that's what I was told. What I remember are the sparks that flew right before everything went dark purple. I got off the field somehow, and Margo's dad took me home in his van.

As we went, I kept looking at my feet. Who took off my soccer shoes and put on my regular sneaks? It bothered me that I couldn't remember.

Margo's dad helped me to the door while Margo walked sideways up the porch steps, chirping cheerful things into my ear. "You're fine," she said. "By tomorrow, you'll feel perfect. Just a little bump. You'll be okay."

My head hurt real bad.

Mom opened the door. Her jaw dropped, and her eyes widened, while Margo and her dad told her what happened. I kept wondering about my soccer shoes, but it was too much work to talk about it.

Mom disappeared into the house for a second before coming out again with her keys. Margo's dad led me by the arm, back down the porch steps, and settled me in our van. And Mom drove me to the emergency room.

All the way there, she said the same chirpy things Margo had said. "You'll be okay. The doctor will fix you right up. You'll see."

After the hospital—mild concussion—Mom draped a throw across me on the couch and sat next to me there, up against my hip all the rest of the day, talking to me and singing to me, and sometimes just sitting in the quiet with me. Deanna came in, too, and did her homework on the floor to keep me company while Mom made dinner.

It felt so good to have them right there for me.

Mom brought dinner out to the coffee table, and all three of us ate around it together. Creamed tuna on rice. My favorite dinner. I wasn't very hungry, but my head wasn't hurting as much by then.

"I wish I knew how I ended up in my sneakers," I remarked. "I can't remember."

"Margo said you did that yourself," Mom said.

Whoa. That slowed me down. "I did it?"

"You'll remember tomorrow," Mom said. "It'll come back."

Deanna said, "Yeah, it'll all come back. Don't worry about it."

With them saying it, I felt a little better.

After dinner, Mom asked Deanna to do the dishes so she could stay with me. And Deanna did, even though it was my turn to do them.

"You'll be all right, Suzie." Mom stroked my hand. "Your sister and I are taking good care of you."

That made me feel so good. What a great family we were!

❋ ❋ ❋

Someone's crying. I check the brown dot in the box. No, not me. I'm just sitting there with those brown walls pressing and pressing.

But . . .

"Ohhh-huhuhuhuhuhhhh . . ."

So heartbreaking, I can't stay in my cloud. So sad in my brown, damp box.

But it's not me.

"Huhuhuhuhhhh . . ."

It's someone sitting at the table by the window.

Karen.

Karen cries? I look again to be sure. It is Karen. Her head with all those tiny little curls is in her arms, and her thin shoulders jump up and down with her sobs. Whatever could make Karen cry?

"Huhuhuhhh . . ."

Karen's voice is pure and full, like the deepest red in a sunlit stained-glass window. How it pierces! Nothing grates at all, but I hate the sound. What happened to her? Did someone die? Can't someone help her?

Jody is there, too, bent over Karen and whispering. But Karen shakes her head and cries louder.

"No one likes me-ee-ee-ee . . ."

"Okay, honey," says Jody.

Jody lifts her like she's a baby, and I see Karen's face. It isn't mean. Her eyes are round and sad. She sees me, and I flinch. What will she do to me?

But she acts like she doesn't care whether I'm there or not. Limp like a rag doll, she doesn't fight, doesn't scream. She only cries, like she's lost everything in the world. Jody carries her out of the room, and the sound softens. Now I don't hear it.

"Wow." It's Joshua, from across the room. His eyes are wide, too. "What happened to her, Edgar?"

Edgar shakes his head. "She's going through a bad time."

The room is silent as everyone draws except me. Karen's paper is where she left it, covered with heavy black arrows, and the black crayon lies crumbled and broken in the center of it.

I take a crayon, but I can think of nothing to draw but big red circles that never touch.

From my bench under the weeping willow tree, I see Kenny help Deanna out of the yellow car on the other side of the fence. She stands with him for a moment, talking. I love her black hair, the way it catches the light. But it's short! Why'd she cut it like that? Deanna loved her long hair.

Then I see her hands and arms. Below the elbow, they're bandaged. It makes mine achy to see that. Now she comes through the gate. I smile at her, but she's shaking her head and frowning.

"Listen," she says, still ten feet away. Her words are all rushy. "I've got to talk to someone, and you can't talk, so you won't tell anyone else."

She sits down on the bench and leans toward me, her blue eyes all shiny. The moment is so intense, I have to look away.

Stella's playing catch with a little boy named Perry. Karen's sitting on a boulder with her knees up at her chest, watching the duck pond, and some other people are playing basketball by the gate. If you didn't know better, you wouldn't think we were all crazy.

"Suzie." Deanna holds up her hands. "Mom did this to me."

What? My heartbeat quickens. *What are you saying?*

"Like with you."

Like me?

"She pushed me against the stove, and my hair went right up in flames."

I shiver like I'm cold, and my heart beats hard against my chest.

No. Mom couldn't have done it.

"Just like that. I burned my hands trying to beat it out. Then I put my head in the sink. Dirty dishes and all." She stands up and strides back and forth, back and forth in front of the bench, holding her arms stiff. "I should have left the house. That's what you have to do when Mom starts pacing and banging things around. You know that. But I was reading, and I forgot to pay attention. That's the key. If you pay attention, you're all right. I should have known better."

Something I'm holding down as hard as I can pushes higher and higher out of my gut. I want to scream, but I hold it in.

Deanna sits down again.

"I went into the kitchen Saturday—yesterday. Just to get a drink of water." Deanna's voice cracks. She pauses to clear her throat. "I saw the dishes from breakfast. I was supposed to wash them. I shouldn't have forgotten. I didn't mean to, I just did. So I started to fill the sink with water, thinking I'd work really fast and maybe Mom wouldn't notice. But she came in before I could do anything. She was so mad. She pushed me right up against the stove. The burner under the teakettle was on."

Deanna stops talking and just shakes her head, staring into space, almost like she's lost her words.

Mom couldn't have done this, I know that. Mom loves Deanna. But Deanna's hands are burned, and her hair is short. No! Mom didn't do this. But Deanna says so. How could Mom—

Oh, Deanna, how could she do this to you?

She looks at me sharply, almost like she's angry with me for saying something.

"Mom didn't mean to hurt me," she says. "She helped me with my hair, and she said she was sorry." She pauses. "We told the emergency room doctor that I tripped and fell against the stove. That's what Mom told Dad, too, when they talked on the phone. Maybe I really did. I don't know. It happened so fast. I can be clumsy. Anyway, the doctor asked me a lot of questions, but I convinced him. Why not? Why would I lie?"

Why? Why?

I reach up to touch the black hair that matches my eyes. It's so soft under my shaking fingers. But red streaks and blisters mark Deanna's neck. She's lucky that's all she has.

I drop my hand into my lap and look into Deanna's eyes. I want so much to say something.

"It'll grow back," she says quickly, reassuringly. "It'll be okay."

I shake my head, tears falling, falling. The thing in my gut is choking me, making my chest hurt.

"Now, don't start," she says. "I'm okay. I just had to tell someone. Anyway, it's my own fault." She smiles kind of sheepishly. "I sure won't forget to do the dishes again."

Dishes! Oh, Deanna.

"How are you doing, anyway?" Deanna asks. "Are you feeling any better?"

I look at her. Right now, I feel awful.

"Don't you worry about me, Suzie. I'm fine." Her voice is high and cheery, but I don't believe her. "You just keep getting better."

Honk, honk! A horn blares from the parking lot.

"That's Kenny," says Deanna. "I have to go now." She stands up, and I stand with her. "Kenny has to be at work soon, but he said he could bring me here if we'd keep it short." She lets out a deep breath. "I had to see you."

She gives me a careful hug and looks down at me with an almost-normal smile. I try to smile back, but I can't.

"Bye, Suzie. I'll stay longer next time."

Deanna leaves, walking through the gates of St. Dorothy's to Kenny's car. Deanna. Her arms with those white bandages on the ends don't swing with her stride. I know she's holding them still because they hurt. I feel the hurt along with her, the way piano strings vibrate together.

My heart races and races. I can't get my breath, and my ears ring, ring, ring. I watch Kenny help Deanna into her seat, then start the car and pull it into the street. I watch until the yellow car with my sister sitting in the passenger seat turns the corner and disappears. Then I watch the last spot I saw her. I saw her. I SAW HER!

BUT NOT DEANNA!

If I'd been there, if I'd only been—if I was—if I was—

I . . . WAS . . . THERE!

My hair, my hair, my hair!

My hair, my skin, my hands—all burning! Someone's screaming and screaming, and I can't breathe. I'm on the floor. My mother hits me all over, not just where the burning is, banging my head on the hard tile.

Now the towel. I'm wrapped in it, and it's over. Everything is quiet, except I'm sobbing and sobbing and sobbing, wishing I could put my hurt head against my hating mother's breast.

Why, why, why?

A choking smell. Smoke. Charred, black cookies on the cookie sheet.

I burned the cookies. After Mom's big argument with Uncle Elliot. They burned. Last February.

Cookies.

Oh, my God.

"Suzie."

I open my eyes. I'm on the grass, and Stella's kneeling over me. The smell of burned cookies, burned hair, burned skin closes in on me. I shut my eyes, feeling it all again like a blanket of hurting, smothering heat.

"No, no, no! Noooooo!" Someone is screaming. It's me! I sit up.

Something cool touches my hand. "Suzie."

It's quiet. I open my eyes again. I see the weeping willow tree overhead, yellow sun lacing through. I feel grass under my legs. Not the kitchen. Quiet. Safe.

"Suzie."

I bring my eyes down. Everyone in the world is staring at me. I feel clammy and feverish and sick to my stomach. Is this a nightmare? I wish.

"Suzie." That's Stella's voice, and I try to focus on her, kneeling at my side, holding my hand. I have to tell her!

Suddenly, all the words I ever heard rush between my ears on a roaring tidal wave. I hear them, but they're so loud and mixed up and muddy that I can't catch the right ones.

A beautiful blue-black butterfly flits by. As black as Deanna's hair. As blue as her eyes.

I point to it. Stella looks from it to me, puzzled. Perry, the boy who was playing catch with Stella, chases it, but it's gone.

The dizzying whirlwind in my head slows down, slows down, until it's a mutter. The words are plainer, easier to find. My tongue unlocks from the roof of my mouth.

"Deanna's hair," I choke out between sobs. "Burned. Burned. Burned."

The storm in my head dies away. All is still.

Scared, so scared. I want to go home. I have to go home. Deanna's in danger.

I want to say this to Stella, but all I can say is, "Burned. Burned. Burned." I show her my hands. "Burned." No other words come.

Karen squats down next to Stella and stares at me.

"Your hands were burned?" Stella asks.

I nod.

"Deanna was burned, too?"

I nod again.

"In the last couple of days?"

Again.

"Someone did it to her?"

I look down. I can't say this, even with a nod. But I have to.

I lift my eyes and nod again.

"Someone you know?

Yes.

"Your father?"

No.

"Your mother?"

I can't answer this. I can't! I can't! She's my mother!

"Your mother did it, didn't she?" insists Stella, but gently. "She burned your hands, too. Am I right? Please tell me."

I hold my hands over my face. My mother will hurt me. I can't do this.

"Why are you hiding, Suzie?" asks Karen. "I'm not going to hurt you. Stella, why's she doing that?"

Stella strokes Karen's hair. "This time it's not about you, Karen. She's afraid of someone else."

Karen's face gets serious. Then she leaves to sit on her boulder to stare at the pond again. Except for Joshua and Stella, the other people have left already.

"Suzie." Stella's voice is soft. "Is it your mother? She hurt you and your sister? It's safe to tell me. Trust me."

Trust. I do trust Stella. I nod at her through my fingers.

My mother burned me, and now she burned Deanna, too.

I cringe, waiting, but nothing happens.

"Oh, Suzie," says Joshua. "This is the worst."

"I agree," says Stella. "I'll call Child Welfare about your sister right away."

Good. So good. I feel better. Deanna will be safe. But—

"You're all right, Suzie. You're still safe," Stella says. She and Joshua help me to my feet, holding my elbows, and we walk to the steps together.

My heart's not racing, and I can breathe. The ringing in my ears has stopped, and I can hear traffic from the street and shouts from the basketball game and the shifting leaves of the weeping willow tree.

I'm all right. Stella says so. I'm all right.

* * *

I'm sitting on the bench with my knees at my chin and my hands over my face, my eyes squinched tight. The box presses so hard that I hurt all over. No matter how I crunch my body, it crushes me. I can't get small enough.

My mother is coming to yell at me. She's going to yell so loud my ears will hurt, my eyes will hurt, my skin will burn. And she will hit me. She will knock me right off the bench, and she will hit and hit and hit until I am pounded right into the ground.

Why did I tell? Why did Deanna tell me? Why did it have to happen?

Mom's not here yet, but I feel her hitting and hear her yelling. It burns and burns and it goes on forever.

I sit as quietly as I can, so I won't bother her, so she'll love me.

But she never will.

No matter how quietly I sit, my mother will never love me. All the hitting and burning and horrible words cannot keep me from knowing this. They used to be able to. I had to concentrate so much on the hurting that I couldn't think past it. I didn't want to. Then I could still believe. I wish it was still that way.

I would invite the pain, concentrate on it, love it, give in to it, die for it if I could think she might love me. Because now, the light shines on this awful, ugly truth. I can't unknow it. I don't want to know it. But it's right there, like the sun in the sky. Only a blind man or a liar could deny the sun. I'm neither, but I want to be both.

It's because of Deanna that I see the truth. How could Mom hurt Deanna like that? Deanna, the person everyone loves.

Who couldn't love Deanna?

Mom.

She must not love her if she could do what she did. Then . . . she must not love me, either. This thought sneaks in through the back door of my mind. Once it's there, it'll never leave. I know this.

The hitting and burning go on, but they fade, dropping like yesterday's floodwaters. I feel the hurts, but they cannot pour over and hide the immovable, iron truth.

"Suzie."

Joshua's quiet voice reaches me through the slowly receding hurts. His "Suzie" is like the click of an electric light switch. The pounding and screaming stop. All is quiet. The leaves overhead rustle in the breeze that tugs at my hair. I open my eyes. It's a bright afternoon. A game of basketball goes on at the hoop over by the gate.

How can they play at a time like this?

Slowly, I put my hands down. I drop my rear end onto the seat and let my feet hang over the grass.

My mother isn't here. I feel her presence and tense up. I remind myself that she isn't here. I feel her again and tense up. I remind myself again. And again. She isn't here. She really isn't.

Joshua is. He's watching me.

"Pretty hard, huh?" he asks.

Pretty hard.

"I called Child Welfare again," says Stella. "They're looking into what happened to your sister's hands. They may take your sister away from your mother."

I knew this would happen. What will happen to Deanna? To my mother? To me? Dad—I don't know. He's such a shadow all the time. Even when he's home, he's hardly there.

"Making us understand about Deanna took a lot of courage."

Colors and feelings fill my mind, but the words they mean dance and tumble on distant waves. I can't answer.

"None of this is your fault, you know," she adds. "You and your sister are victims."

Well, there's knowing, and there's knowing. My gut doesn't exactly agree with my head on this. Like fitting a round peg into a square hole.

"I'm sorry." Stella's eyes are round and sad.

Sorry for what? For getting my mother into trouble? For rescuing Deanna? She can't be sorry about that. I'm not—not about Deanna. She'll be safe. But my mother. Stella's sorry my mother doesn't love me. That's the big sorry.

I don't want it to be true. That's the problem. I want to believe that she loves me, that she just isn't very good at showing it.

But she doesn't show it because she doesn't feel it. And even if, somewhere in her heart, under all her layers of other things, she does love me, nothing is different. The hurts are still the hurts. It doesn't matter what you call it.

You would think a person who sings like an angel could love her daughter. You would think that if her songs made her daughter's heart sing, she'd naturally love her daughter. How can she sound like that and not love? But the two don't necessarily go together.

I hate knowing this.

But here's the funny thing. The more I let myself believe the truth, the better I feel.

It's not my fault that she doesn't love me. There's something wrong with Mom. Stella keeps telling me that, and part of me knows she's right. It's that other part of me that argues back about it, but Stella says these things take time to settle in your bones.

Mom hurt Deanna, the same way she hurt me. If Mom loved us, she couldn't have hurt us. It's not Deanna's fault. It's not my fault. We never made Mom hurt us.

I don't have to sit on the chair, quiet, so quiet. It won't get me Mom's love.

Why else do it?

I stand up and walk to the window. I look past the gates at the end of St. Dorothy's drive to the streets and houses, the trees, the blue sky. I want to be out in that world.

Stella watches out the window with me. "It's tough right now," she says, "but you're going to be fine."

*** ❋❋❋

I walk out to see the ducks. There are people around, but no one's watching, not really. I guess someone will notice if I jump into the water. They won't let me drown. But I'm not going to jump into the water.

I kneel down by the shore of the pond. The ducks swim or sleep, ignoring me. I could be a twig or a blade of grass, I'm so interesting. Then I tear a piece of bread from the slice I took at lunch. I throw it into the water. I throw another and another. With each piece I throw, my heart feels lighter. It feels so good to tear and throw, tear and throw, I wish I had a whole loaf. The ducks stop pretending they don't see me and charge after the crumbs.

Quack-quack-quack-quack! I am surrounded by ducks. Some even come up onto the bank. I have no more bread.

I say one of my words. "Sorry."

I laugh at saying "Sorry" to the begging, squawking, well-fed ducks who treated me like a twig a minute ago. I laugh and I laugh, collapsing onto the grass. The sun warms my face, the grass tickles my ears. The ducks leave to quack and splash, now disgusted with me. And I laugh.

"Suzie?"

Behind me is a bunch of people—Jody, Stella, and Joshua among them. Their faces are so worried. Suzie—laughing?

I can hardly stand up. My body is shaking from laughing so hard. I point to the ducks and search for a word among the millions.

"Funny," I say.

"Funny?" asks Stella.

"Funny?" asks Joshua. "The ducks are funny?"

I laugh some more. Gradually, the worried faces loosen into smiles. My friends are no longer afraid I've completely lost my mind.

Funny.

***

In my room with the door closed, I practice my words.

"Funny. Sorry. Deanna's hair." I say them over and over. Then I say another that I think I own. "Friend. Friend."

I sit on the bed. It takes too much work to stand when I'm trying words.

I try the words in a different order.

"Deanna's hair. Sorry. Funny. Friend."

Then I try to catch other words. I know they're out there, but I have to find each of them like a photographer finds his picture. Zoom in and focus.

"Joshua . . . friend. Ducks . . . funny. Deanna's hair . . . sorry. Deanna, I'm sorry." The words don't come fast or easy, but they come. I can find them.

"Joshua is my friend. The ducks are funny. I love Deanna." Then suddenly, I know. All the words I want are right there.

I jump up from my bed. Words! I have words!

I run out of my room.

"Joshua, Joshua, Joshua!" I yell. My voice echoes in the wide hall. "Ducks are funny!"

Jody stares at me as I open the main door. I see the beginning of an amazed smile, but I don't wait for the rest of it.

"Joshua!" I yell from the top step.

At his name, he stops kicking the soccer ball. He stares at me. The ball goes on until it hits the fence.

"Joshua, Joshua, Joshua!" I jump down a step each time I shout his name.

He runs to meet me as I land on the bottom step. I grab his hands. His face is all lit up, just like mine must be.

"Joshua, I have words!"

❋❋❋

Joshua has gone home for good. He's all finished here. He says he'll call me on the telephone sometimes or visit me. He gave me his phone number and address. I'm glad I have some words, so I can talk to him when he calls.

He gets to be at home. Play soccer for his team. That's wonderful.

I used to think that if I stopped crying, I could go home. I stopped crying. I sleep sometimes without help. I'm talking pretty well. Not great. It's kind of like my foot-dragging was. I have to really think about it. And most of the time, I don't sit with my knees up at my chin. That's a hard habit to break. But I can't go home.

I have no home. Not since Stella found out about the fire.

"Where can I go?" I ask her.

She looks at me with those sorrowful green eyes.

"We're working on it," she says.

But wherever I go, it won't be the same. I don't know how I feel about that. After all, I really don't want to go back to sitting quietly. That was my job. At least, I thought so. But I will miss Mom singing and Dad snoring and Deanna's friends laughing and raiding the refrigerator. No more knock-knock jokes with Tony or some other boyfriend.

Knock knock.

Who's there?

***

Deanna comes to see me. Her short hair is all curly with a permanent.

Aunt Olga and Uncle Elliot are here, too. They give me a bunch of black-eyed Susans before they move to a sofa by one of the windows. I always liked black-eyed Susans. When I was little, I thought they were named after me.

Aunt Olga and Uncle Elliot can see us, but they're not close enough to hear. They're nice to let me visit with Deanna alone.

"They took me away from Mom," says Deanna. "You told. I don't know how you did it."

Her voice is accusing.

"Sorry," I say. I reach out to Deanna's hair.

Deanna stares at me for a minute, not quite sure she heard. Then she brushes my hand away. She winces when her bandaged hand touches mine.

"It'll grow back." Her voice is impatient. "It would have been all right. We just had to learn to pay better attention and not make Mom mad. But now it's too late."

I am sorry, in a way. But Deanna's safe. That's good.

"I'm glad you're safe," I say.

Deanna stares at me again. She knows she heard me this time.

"You're talking." Her face gets all red. At first I can't tell whether she's mad or what. "You're talking. Oh, Suzie, you're talking!" I know she'd be bouncing up and down if it

157

weren't for her hands. She looks past me. "Uncle Elliot, Aunt Olga, she's talking." She puts her arms carefully around my neck. "That's the most wonderful thing in the whole world. I'm so happy."

She lets go, and then she hugs me again.

"If you're talking, then everything's going to be fine. I know it is."

"Yes," I say. "Yes." It's the only word I can find. "Yes."

"They made me tell them about the time you were burned. They know all about that now."

The memory hits me like a sudden, fierce thunderclap.

My hands are on my face, beating at the flames. I fall off my chair to roll on the floor, anything to put out the fire. My breath comes fast and raspy. My ears ring almost as loud as my scream.

"You're okay!" Deanna is shouting from overhead. "There's no fire! You're okay! Stop, now! Stop!"

The realness of the fire falls away. I stop screaming. I stop screaming and discover that I'm lying on the cool blue-and-white floor of the solarium at St. Dorothy's. How many times am I going to do this?

Deanna is squatting beside me. Over and over, she's saying, softly now, "You're okay. You're fine. You're safe."

I don't remember the chair tipping over, but it's on its side next to me.

Deanna touches my arm with her bandaged hands. I know she wants to help me up, but her hands are too sore. I sit up on my own.

"Mom won't hurt us now," I say.

"No," says Deanna. "We're safe. I guess that's what's important." She says it like she's not quite sure.

I see Stella and my aunt and uncle, all with worried faces, bent over us. Karen's behind them. Her face isn't mad. Her eyes are wide and round, scared. Why is she scared? She *likes* me to be scared. Our eyes connect, and she disappears behind Stella.

I get up by myself and pick up the chair. Shake my head, still feeling the nightmare air.

"She . . . she was remembering February," Deanna says.

I nod.

Uncle Elliot looks mad. "If I'd only known . . . but your mother wouldn't let me in the house. I could have—"

I interrupt him. "It was a secret. A bad one."

He nods and looks as though he'd like to say a lot more, but he doesn't.

He and the other grown-ups make sure I'm okay before they move back to where they'd been. I *guess* I'm okay. Sometimes my hands still hurt, but the marks are gone. The ones you can see.

"I had to tell," I say to Deanna. "I couldn't stand you being burned."

"I know, but well—" She tries to wipe her eyes with the part of her bandage nearest her elbows, but she can't quite reach the tears. I take a tissue from a nearby box and wipe them off for her. That makes her smile. "Always looking out for me," she says. "But listen, Suzie. Mom's in so much trouble. Couldn't you have just—" She breaks off, her voice a squeak.

"I couldn't," I say. "Not anymore."

Deanna stares at me for a minute. "I don't understand why you couldn't if I could," she says. "But I guess you couldn't."

"Look at your hands," I say, as gently as I can.

She does, then looks back at me. "But it's Mom, Suzie.

"Yes. It's Mom."

We sit without talking, just being together. We're sad, but we're all right.

"Mom needs help," Deanna says suddenly. "That's what Uncle Elliot and Aunt Olga keep telling me. I'm staying with them for now, maybe longer."

"Uncle Elliot and Aunt Olga?" I look at their kindly faces.

"They want you to come, too," she adds. "Anytime you're ready."

I look around the solarium, at my aunt and uncle, at Stella, at the jigsaw puzzle boxes, at the weeping willow tree outside, weaving in the glowing sunlight.

"I'm ready."

***

I'm leaving in the morning. My suitcases are all packed, and I'm ready to go. I sit on my bed, remembering my first night here when I couldn't sleep and hardly knew my own name. Doesn't seem exactly real anymore. When things are so bad, I guess it's hard to believe in them afterwards.

Knock-knock-knock.

I open my door. Karen's there. I push the door to close it. Karen's one person I won't miss.

"Wait," she says. "Jody's with me." She turns and points. Jody is there—near, but not too near.

"What do you want?" I come out into the hall and shut the door. Jody or no Jody, I don't want Karen in my room.

"Remember that day in the solarium when you laughed?" Karen asks. "I asked you what was funny. Would you tell me?"

"Why should I tell you anything?" I am so angry with this girl. "You ripped my picture and broke my mirror. You hit or kick me every chance you get. Forget it. I'm not telling you anything."

Karen lowers her eyes.

"Look," she says after a second. "Can you please tell me what was funny? I really need to know. Please."

Here's something else funny. I feel sorry for Karen. Something is really wrong with her. Not that I'll let her push me around again.

I hesitate. "It won't mean anything to you."

She looks up again. Her face isn't angry the way it usually is, just miserable. "I need to know something funny. Please. Nothing's happy or funny to me. It's all gray."

"Well . . ." I hesitate once more, but then I remember my time of gravel-gray damp. "Sure. It won't hurt to tell you. I was humming."

"I know. I heard you."

"That's all it was—trying out sounds without words. Talking without talking is what I thought it was."

"What does that mean? Talking without talking?"

"Just . . . nothing. I was afraid of talking, I guess. It can get you into trouble. So I was talking without words. It's not really funny. You don't have to laugh at it."

Karen frowns, thinking. "I just wish I understood. I'll never get out of here. What's getting you out?"

I bite my lower lip. Do I want to tell her? Well, I guess it doesn't matter, really. I'm leaving tomorrow. And I do feel sorry for her.

"My mother did something really bad to me," I begin.

Pain flashes across Karen's face and is gone. I know it slices her right to the heart, even though the only place it shows is in the darkness of her eyes. How much work is it to hide that much pain? But I know about this.

"I had to talk about it," I say. "When I could, things got better."

"My father . . ." Karen's voice trails off. She looks off to the side, and her eyes get even darker. She can't say it—not to me.

"Try," I say.

Karen shakes her head real fast. "You don't know," she says. "I can't. Besides, there's nothing to tell."

"You can," I say. "You just don't know it yet, that's all."

Karen's shoulders are hunched. Her head is downcast.

"I could stand it if only everything wasn't so gray."

Her voice, rounded by despair, pierces my heart. The anguish! I can hardly bear it. Without thinking, I put my arms around Karen's thin shoulders. She sighs and buries her eyes under my collarbone. Fragile. That's what Karen is. Not tough.

"Wait," I say.

I slip into my room and return with the peacock feathers.

"Here." She needs them more than I do. "Peacock feathers are never gray."

She stares, first at the feathers, then at me, just like Deanna did before. She takes them.

"—nks." She can hardly say it, I can tell, but it's enough. She doesn't move at all for a long time. "I was scared when you had that fit in the solarium. You know why?"

"Why?"

"I thought you were going crazy again. I couldn't stand you being pulled back down." She strokes the feathers against her face. "You're so strong, and the monster was getting you again. That's what I thought. I'm not as strong as you are. If you can't get away from the monster, I sure can't."

"You kill the monster with words," I say. "The words are yours. Use them."

Karen half turns, then stops to look back. Unshed tears

make her eyes shine. "I'm sorry about your mirror and your picture."

"It's all right," I say.

Karen's slow stride weaves slightly as she walks away. Jody takes her by the arm, and I hear a loud sob after they turn down the next hall.

Oh, Karen!

Almost Thanksgiving, and a chilly wind blows the dry leaves around my feet as I get out of Uncle Elliot's car. Aunt Olga gets out of the car and—right away—gasps. I look up. Mom's here. She's sitting on the bottom porch step in front of Aunt Olga's and Uncle Elliot's house.

"I know, I know," says Mom to my aunt and uncle, "but I thought you could forgive one minute."

Next thing, I'm hugging her like I'll never see her again. I've missed her so much.

"It's okay, honey," she whispers through my hair. She strokes my shoulders, and it feels so right. "It's all going to be just fine."

Then I detach myself partly, my hands resting on her arms. "But . . ."

"I'm going to AA again," she says. "I'm not going to drink anymore. Ever. I promise."

"But . . ."

"Here." She thrusts something at me. A sweater. It's what she was crocheting the last time I saw her. Something for me! I put it on. "I always thought green was your color," she says. "Makes your hair shine."

"I love it!"

"A welcome-home present." She looks up at Uncle Elliot's and Aunt Olga's house. "Well . . . sort of."

Uncle Elliot edges closer.

I look at Mom's eyes. She looks at mine. Her eyes tell me

she's sorry, but she doesn't say it. Something makes me think she doesn't know how.

"I better go," she says.

I hug her tight one more time. She kisses me on the cheek. It feels so good that for one moment, everything is fixed, and I'm ready to start pretending again. Only for that one moment, though.

Then she's in her car, waving, and she's gone.

"Are you all right?" asks Uncle Elliot.

"Beautiful sweater," says Aunt Olga.

"I'm all right," I say. "I'm glad she's trying. Maybe she'll be okay. Maybe Deanna and I can live with her again. Maybe."

Maybe not, too. That's what my heart says.

We climb up the steps to my new home.

I'm at the kitchen table at Aunt Olga's and Uncle Elliot's. Deanna and I are eating ice cream. A spoon carefully held with Deanna's bandaged fingers brings butter pecan up to her lips. She smiles at me over the bandage.

She answers my unasked question. "Feels better every day. I can always find a way to eat ice cream."

Mine is strawberry—the kind with those big frozen chunks. Fantastic! How wonderful when you can ask for things!

My aunt and uncle stir their coffee, sip it some. Mostly, they're smiling at each other and at us.

It feels good to be here.

Uncle Elliot says Dad will be in and out like always. Deanna and I can't see Mom for awhile. Uncle Elliot says Mom's getting counseling plus the AA stuff, so maybe things will work out. Maybe. But I don't know how I'll ever feel safe with her.

And Margo's coming over tomorrow. At first, she didn't say anything at all when I called. Then she screamed "Yippee!" so loud Deanna could hear Margo's voice on the phone from the next room. Deanna came in and grinned wide.

The box doesn't press so hard on me anymore, but I'm still in it. Everything isn't perfect yet. Why should it be? You can't fix everything overnight. That's what Stella says. But I'm going to keep working at it, no matter how long it takes.

Then watch this eagle soar . . .

Susan Shaw is a native Pennsylvanian and a graduate of Temple University. She and her husband live in Wayne, Pennsylvania, where they raised three children. Ms. Shaw is the author of both *The Boy from the Basement*, which the New York Public Library chose as one of its Books for the Teen Age, and the newly released *Safe*. *Black-eyed Suzie* is her first published novel.